THE FRYEBURG CHRONICLES
BOOK IV
Journeys From Home

By JUNE O'DONAL

Copyright © 2016 by June O'Donal

The Fryeburg Chronicles Book IV
Journeys From Home
by June O'Donal

Printed in the United States of America.

ISBN 9781498475433

All rights reserved solely by the author. The author guarantees all contents are original and do not infringe upon the legal rights of any other person or work. No part of this book may be reproduced in any form without the permission of the author. The views expressed in this book are not necessarily those of the publisher.

Unless otherwise indicated, Scripture quotations taken from the King James Version (KJV) – *public domain*.

www.xulonpress.com

"The fear of the Lord is the beginning of knowledge:
But fools despise wisdom and instruction."
Proverbs 1:7

Acknowledgements

I am indebted to my coworkers at The Remick Country Doctor Museum and Farm in Tamworth, NH for teaching me about herbal remedies, general stores, historic cooking and recipes, historic games and toys and one-room school houses. I thank the Fryeburg Public Library for an endless supply of interlibrary loan books and the Fryeburg Historical Society's research library for sharing their energy and resources.

Barbara Hill, archivist for Fryeburg Academy, located some sources on the fire in 1851. Tour guide Donald Guillerault provided me a first-hand look at the immense brick buildings of the Biddeford Textile Mill and shared fascinating anecdotes. Thank you to my husband, Wayne, for encouraging me to finish this project after my cancer diagnosis and long treatment.

About the Cover

I purchased this oil painting twenty-three years ago from the artist, retired Reverend Gordon Nichols. I often wondered, is this solitary figure leaving home or returning…

The Table of Contents

Acknowledgements................................v
The Miller Family Tree...........................ix

I.	The Millers 11
II.	Journey from Ireland 20
III.	Saturday on the Farm 28
IV.	Keeping the Sabbath..................... 39
V.	Journey to Buffalo 47
VI.	Karl Marx.............................. 55
VII.	The General Store...................... 60
VIII.	Journey to Biddeford 69
IX.	The Boarding House..................... 84
X.	The Textile Mill 93
XI.	Life without Rachel 106
XII.	The Sawyer 120
XIII.	The Fight 128
XIV.	Journey Home 139
XV.	The Proprietress....................... 152
XVI.	Just a Farmer 162
XVII.	Journey from California................ 170
XVIII.	Fire!................................. 178
XIX.	Final Journey 187

Fryeburg Landmarks............................. 195
Discussion Questions 201
End Notes 203
Bibliography................................... 209

Miller Family Tree

I. James Miller and Sarah Bradford Miller
  A. Micah Miller born 1764, died 1848–married Grace Peabody in 1785
     1. Elizabeth (Libby) Peabody Miller born 1786 married with four children and lived in Boston.
     2. Sarah (Sadie) Alden Miller born 1788
     3. William Peabody Miller born 1792, died 1792
     4. Alden James Miller born 1794 – married with children lived in Buffalo
  B. **Benjamin James Miller** born 1767 married Hannah Chase in 1793
     1. **Jacob Freeman Miller** born 1794 married Katherine (Kate) Wiley in 1813
        a. **Elijah (Eli) James Miller** born 1814 married Julia Frye Miller
           1. Rebecca (Becky) Miller born 1838
           2. Victoria Miller born 1840
           3. David (Davy) Miller born 1843
        b. **Daniel (Danny) Chase Miller** born 1816 married Emily Walker
        c. **Rachel Miller** born 1820
        d. **Isaac Miller** born 1838
     2. **Abigail Miller** born in 1796 married Joshua Pierce in 1824
        a. **Thaddeus Pierce** born in 1825

I
The Millers

Grace and Hannah Miller, sisters-in-law and best friends, strolled down Main Street of Fryeburg Village, Maine stopping to observe the construction of the new Congregational Church.

Grace asked, "Did I ever tell you about the first time the Millers took me to church back in 1781? It met in Isaac Abbott's home, because the meeting house did not have heat."[1]

"A thousand times," Hannah replied patiently.

"Did I ever tell you when I was growing up in Boston my family attended North Church? It was a beautiful, brick, Anglican Church with a white spire reaching to the heavens and a brass chandelier imported from England.[2] Our family pew was just two rows behind the Royal Governor's before he was forced to leave with the other Loyalists back in 1776?"

"A thousand and one times," Hannah laughed.

"It seems like only yesterday," Grace sighed.

"It was more like seventy-two years ago," Hannah corrected.

"Good afternoon, ladies," Reverend Hurd warmly greeted the octogenarians. "It is a lovely May afternoon for a walk."

"We are admiring your church," Grace replied.

"It is not my church. It is the Lord's church," he explained. "It will have two columns in the front and a hundred-foot-tall steeple with a clock."³ He hoped that he was not boasting. "I know it will not be as elegant as your North Church in Boston," he smiled at Grace, "or as simple as your Quaker meeting house back in Philadelphia," he turned to Hannah.

"Sir, you truly know us too well!" Hannah laughed.

"It is indeed my pleasure to know you and your families. Enjoy your walk," the good pastor doffed his hat and headed to the parsonage.

The ladies continued and paused in front of Fryeburg Academy, a two story wooden structure capped with a belfry and bell. Not only did this bell call scholars to class during the week, it called the faithful to worship on Sunday mornings.⁴ Hannah's husband, Benjamin served as the first preceptor when the school opened back in 1792. Over the decades he was also the first attorney in town, a judge and United States senator. Now retired, he devoted much of his time as a trustee of the academy.

"Let us stop at the general store on our way home," Grace suggested. As the daughter of a wealthy Boston merchant she enjoyed surveying the merchandise that was randomly displayed in every nook and corner. This elderly extrovert relished the greetings of her neighbors and the gossip of the village. An eclectic collection of aromas greeted them as they entered the crowded store. Grace inhaled deeply savoring the smells of tobacco, coffee and spices.

Mr. Evans, the proprietor, welcomed them. "Beautiful day for a walk."

"Truly," Hannah agreed. "Has the mail arrived?"

Mr. Evans' thirty-year-old son, Peter informed Grace, "Mrs. Miller, you have received a few letters today." He handed her one letter from her daughter Libby in Boston and one from her son Alden in Buffalo.

"Thank you, Peter." Grace tightly held her treasured correspondence in her hand as she continued to browse. "There is no letter from Thaddeus today," Peter apologized to Hannah.

Thaddeus Pierce was her grandson and the only child of her daughter and son-in-law, Abigail and Joshua Pierce.

An elderly man spat a wad of tobacco into a nearby spittoon as Hannah walked by. "I beg your pardon, Mam." Her views on the "disgusting habit" of chewing tobacco were well known in the village. Hannah smiled courteously. She surveyed the writing paper, pewter ink stand, quills, lead pencils and slates inexplicably displayed near the stoneware crocks of rum and apple whiskey. Mr. Evans smiled apologetically for he knew this gentle, Quaker lady was an active member of the Temperance Society.

Hannah found Grace on the other side of the store eyeing a white lace table cloth and tea set near the chamber pots and brass hinges. "Would you care to stop by for a cup of tea?" Hannah invited. Grace understood this was Hannah's polite way of stating she was ready to head home.

The two approached the front door of the stately Federal-styled, white house on the corner of Main and River Streets. Hannah's son-in-law, Joshua, opened the door and greeted them cheerfully. "Mother, did you enjoy your walk? Aunt Grace, you are looking well. I believe these afternoon excursions agree with you."

Hannah smiled at him in gratitude. Joshua, a considerate and modest man, always had an appropriately kind word. A partner in his father-in-law's law firm, he took over the practice upon Benjamin's retirement. Since his marriage in 1824, the four of them shared this large home and law office. "Abigail is getting the tea for us and Mr. Miller is reading in the front parlor."

Hannah studied the dignified, elderly gentleman dozing on the settee by the front window. She was concerned about his loss of weight and fatigue. After he had fallen a few times this winter she insisted that he use his cane.

"Come in, dear, I have been waiting for you," Benjamin invited.

"I am sorry to have awakened you," she apologized.

"Not at all, I was merely resting my eyes. I enjoy my afternoon tea with my three favorite ladies," he smiled as Abigail set down a pewter tray holding a porcelain teapot, cups and saucers. Although Abigail was a notoriously bad cook, she was a gracious hostess.

"Mama, was there any mail today?" Abigail tried to sound nonchalant. The family was anxiously awaiting word from Thaddeus. This precocious child graduated from Fryeburg Academy at the age of fourteen and from Harvard at eighteen. His work as a reporter for the New York Post sent him all over the United States and Europe. The year 1848 brought much turmoil to Europe and Thaddeus was there reporting on those tumultuous events. He was due home over three months ago. Anxiety creased Abigail's face as she poured the tea.

"Even in this modern day, mail from Europe is simply unreliable. I am confident there is a reasonable explanation for his delay and the letter which explains it has been lost." Benjamin, the attorney spoke logically; Benjamin the grandfather silently worried.

The five of them sipped their tea when the back door opened and slammed.

"Grandpa!" Isaac Miller, Benjamin and Hannah's ten-year-old grandson, called from the kitchen. Isaac, meaning son of laughter, was the perfect name for this much loved child. In the winter of 1838, his father, Jacob, learned that he was to be a grandfather for the first time when his eldest son, Elijah, and his wife, Julia, announced they were expecting. That evening in the privacy of their bedroom Jacob's wife, Kate, revealed that she too was with child.

"How did this happen?" she sobbed.

"I know exactly how this happened," he laughed with joy as he hugged his wife.

"What will people think?" she snapped.

"People will think that the Lord has blessed us in our old age!"

"This is ridiculous! Eli is twenty-four, married and having a child, Danny is twenty-two and married and Rachel is eighteen. What about my business? How am I to care for an infant while making cheese and butter and delivering my goods to the Oxford House and the general store?"

"You will have much help. Aunt Grace and Rachel can run the creamery for a while. Danny's wife Emily, my sister and my mother will help watch the baby. There are plenty of Millers to love and raise this child."

"How was school today?"

"Boring! Grandpa, did you have a good day?"

"I most certainly did. I helped Uncle Joshua prepare for a court case and I am catching up on some reading."

Isaac suddenly remembered the reason he stopped by his grandparents' house. "Sadie is crying in the cemetery again. I tried to take her home, but I do not think she heard me."

Sadie, Grace's middle child, was an artist known for her landscapes, seascapes and portraits. As the wealthiest woman in town, she also owned thousands of acres of prime forest and was the sole proprietor of S.A. Miller Enterprises, a company which sold timbers to saw mills and shipyards.

Many in town thought this middle aged woman was eccentric because she never married nor socialized with people outside of her family. Her loved ones understood that because of a childhood hearing loss she felt uncomfortable with people. She often could not follow conversations and preferred the solitude of her art studio.

No one took the sudden death of her father, Micah Miller, harder than Sadie. She wept uncontrollably at the funeral, visited the cemetery daily and stopped painting entirely.

"Aunt Grace, Abigail and I will get her," Joshua offered. "You sit here and enjoy your tea." Grace nodded gratefully.

Joshua and Abigail entered the Village Cemetery located behind the stone school house and found Sadie sobbing in front of her father's grave.

Micah James Miller
Beloved Son, Brother, Husband and Father
January 5, 1764 – March 9, 1848

Even at the age of eighty-four, this strong and good hearted farmer still milked the cows and groomed his prized horses. He left the planting and field work to his nephew Jacob, and his grandnephew Eli.

One morning Micah loaded the wagon with his sap buckets and spiels as Sadie loaded her paints, easel and canvas. Father and daughter headed out to tap maple trees and to paint. Making maple syrup was still his favorite chore on the farm. Grace was not concerned when Micah and Sadie did not appear for the noon meal. They often lost track of time while engaged in their work. By midafternoon she sent Jacob with a lunch basket to search for them. Jacob found his cousin blissfully painting by the bank of the Saco River and discovered Uncle Micah dead lying face down in the snow guarded by his loyal horses.

"Sadie blames herself for her father's death," Grace confided. "She fears Micah may have called for help and she was unable to hear him and go to his aid."

Abigail gently put her hand on Sadie's shoulder to get her attention. "Come join your mother and us for tea." Joshua firmly took her arm and quietly led Sadie out of the cemetery.

When Joshua and Abigail escorted Sadie into the front parlor, Benjamin motioned to her to sit by him on the settee. "Your father did not fear death. He feared becoming an invalid. I believe that his sudden death was exactly how he would have chosen to go. Of course it was a terrible shock to all of us.

Do you remember the day your grandfather died twenty-nine years ago?" Sadie nodded. "Your father was devastated. Do you know what he did the day after the funeral? He went back outside and planted the fields. He continued farming out of love and respect for his father.

Sadie, you must go on with your life. Honor your father through your painting. You paint landscapes, and you paint portraits. Why not combine them? Why not paint scenes from your father's life – making maple syrup, husking corn, planting the fields, caring for his horses?"

In a rare display of familial affection, Sadie hugged her uncle tightly and kissed him on the cheek. "Thank you, Uncle Benjamin! Papa always said that you were the smartest one in the family!" With a smile, she rose and headed back to the farm and to her studio.

Benjamin swallowed the lump in his throat.

"Thank you, Benjamin. I thank all of you for your comfort since we lost Micah. Isaac, will you be a gentleman and escort your old aunt back home?"

Isaac enjoyed the company of his elderly relatives who lavished him with their undivided attention. During his youngest years he spent his days at his grandparents' house where Benjamin taught him to read and to play chess. Now retired, Benjamin had much time to devote to his youngest grandson. Hannah made his clothes and told him Bible stories. Aunt Grace told and retold exciting stories from her childhood. Sadie gave him a few drawing lessons and lent him some of her quills and ink. Isaac took his great aunt's arm and they slowly headed down the lane to the farm by the river.

Abigail absent-mindedly stirred the pot of soup with one hand as she held a copy of *The Last of the Mohicans* by James Fennimore Cooper in the other. She stopped stirring long enough to turn the page. Ten years ago, Joshua had surprised her with a Glenwood cook stove hoping it would improve her cooking skills. With the ashes contained in the stove, it kept the kitchen cleaner which meant less sweeping and stooping. Foods could conveniently be baked in the oven, rather than buried in ashes on the hearth floor. The stove brought many improvements in life; unfortunately it did not improve Abigail's cooking.

Most meals at the Miller/Pierce household involved animated discussions of politics and current events. However, this evening everyone ate silently lost in their thoughts.

Abigail fought the panic as she visualized every possible disaster her son may have encountered. His ship could have been attacked by pirates as they sailed through the Mediterranean Sea. Perhaps he had been murdered in some back alley in Paris; his unidentified body buried in a paupers' grave. There was civil unrest throughout Europe. What if he was injured in a riot in Rome? What if he was arrested as a spy in Munich? Perhaps he lay dying of cholera in some filthy London hospital. She silently chided herself for her runaway imagination. Her mother may be correct that Abigail read too many novels and not enough Scripture.

Joshua did not wish to upset his wife, but he occasionally felt tremors in his right hand and a tingling sensation in his left leg. Legible penmanship was a necessity for an attorney. He felt the responsibility of being the sole provider of the family, since Benjamin retired. How could he continue to practice law with an unsteady hand? When Thaddeus returns home, he would convince his son that his years of travel were over. It was time to settle down and continue the family law firm. It was extremely inconsiderate of him not to write and to worry his mother.

Hannah admired Grace's determination to continue living her life to the fullest. She glanced at her husband. How could she ever live without Benjamin? Grace had always been a strong, independent woman, with her own wealth, business and opinions. How would Hannah fare as a widow? It was Benjamin who had taught her to read and write back in

Philadelphia. It was Benjamin who brought her to Fryeburg, married her and provided for her. She prayed that the Lord would take her before her husband.

Benjamin stared pensively out of the dining room window. As the patriarch it was his duty to assure every family member would be provided for after he was gone. Of late, he wondered if his time would be sooner than later. His brother Micah's will stipulated that the house was left to Grace and the barns and fields went to his nephew, Jacob. Upon Grace's death the house would then go to Jacob with the stipulation that Sadie would continue to live there. Eli would someday inherit the house and farm from his father.

Benjamin had purchased some property on the Saco River near Walker's Island and built a saw mill. His second grandson, Daniel and his wife Emily Walker Miller now lived in a cozy cottage at the mill and made a handsome living.

His only granddaughter, Rachel, was a beautiful, talented young woman. Someday she would marry and have her own home. If not she would remain at the farm working with her mother in the creamery.

Of course it was expected that Thaddeus would one day return and inherit the house and law firm. But what of Isaac? Would he work on the farm for his brother Eli? Would he work at the saw mill for his brother Daniel? Benjamin's brooding was interrupted by the kitchen door opening and then slamming.

"Am I late for supper?" a familiar voice rang.

"Thaddeus!"

II

Journey from Ireland

"Thaddeus, we have been worried sick about you!" Abigail flung her arms around her son's neck.

"I wrote you from Liverpool, stating I would be visiting Ireland before my return. Did you not receive my letter?"

The family gathered around him plying him with questions. It was Hannah who noticed the boy who appeared to be Isaac's age standing shyly against the wall. He looked uncomfortable in his tweed knickers and jacket, linen shirt and cap.

"Please come in," she invited. "I am Thaddeus' grandmother. Welcome to our home."

"Forgive me. Darian, may I present to you my parents, Mr. and Mrs. Pierce and my grandparents, Mr. and Mrs. Miller. This is Darian Flynn from Ireland."

The boy nodded.

"Why would you want to go to Ireland?" Abigail asked Thaddeus.

"It was not part of my original itinerary. It is a long story. Perhaps I could relay it after I have eaten?"

Darian stood silently staring at the large pot of soup simmering on the cook stove, stoneware crocks lining the shelves in the pantry, slices of bread and a crock of butter set upon the table.

"If I had known you were arriving I would have prepared a more suitable meal," Abigail apologized. Hannah went to the cupboard to retrieve two more bowls and plates.

"How do you like America?" Joshua asked.

"It is very big," Darian replied without taking his eyes off of the soup being ladled into his bowl.

"First we docked in New York where I had several articles to submit. After a few days we sailed to Boston and then Portland," Thaddeus explained with his mouth full. Darian stifled a yawn before grabbing his third piece of bread.

"What is happening in Europe?" Benjamin asked.

"There is unrest everywhere. There were riots in Paris and Louis Philippe abdicated."[1]

"Those French are an unstable lot," Benjamin interjected. "First they beheaded their king and then they crowned Napoleon their emperor. Napoleon brought war and destruction across most of Europe and now more unrest!"

"France is only the beginning. There were riots in Prague, Vienna and Budapest. Hungary is virtually independent. A constitution was promised to the Czechs and Poland is fighting for independence,"[2] Thaddeus continued.

"There appears to be a battle between the old order of monarchy and the rise of nationalism. Minority ethnic groups no longer wish to be part of a larger empire or kingdom. They want their own countries,"[3] Joshua hypothesized.

"The time of feudalism has ended," Benjamin added.

"Yes, and it has been replaced by something far worse," Thaddeus suggested. "Capitalism is the root of all evil."

"The love of money is the root of all evil," Joshua corrected. "Capitalism is neutral; it can be used for good or evil."

Benjamin challenged his grandson. "My father came to Fryeburg before I was born, built a small, two-room house and planted a field. By the end of his lifetime he had a successful farm, a grand barn and a house large enough to shelter his wife, three grown sons, two daughters-in-law and five grandchildren. That farm continues to provide a livelihood for my son, Jacob, and his son, Eli. Where is the evil with that? I began my law firm part-time from the front room of my father's house in 1792" Benjamin explained. "As I gained experience and clients I was able to afford to build my own house and office. As my practice grew, I hired your father as my assistant. Where is the evil in that?"

Thaddeus countered, "You should visit the industrial cities in England. Manchester is filled with textile mills with unsafe working conditions. Men, women and even young children are working long hours at starvation wages. The workers cannot afford decent housing, or adequate food. They call it the Industrial Revolution. Someday soon there will be a real revolution."

Abigail quickly changed the subject. "Darian, you look exhausted. If you are done eating, let me show you to your room and get you settled. We will let the men argue about politics."

When he thought no one was looking, he stole two pieces of bread and hid it under his jacket. Wordlessly he followed her through the formal dining room and front parlor staring at the furniture, draperies, parlor stoves, and oil lamps. He entered the front foyer and eyed the magnificent landscapes gracing the walls. He followed her up the front staircase and passed three bedrooms before arriving at Thaddeus' childhood bedroom.

"I hope you do not mind sharing a bedroom. I am afraid the guest room has been used for storage." She pulled out the trundle bed, put fresh linens and an old quilt upon it. "Thaddeus' grandmother made this quilt for him when he was a little boy," she explained nostalgically. She placed a linen pillowcase on a pillow stuffed with dried corn husks. "Do you need anything?"

Darian looked around at the oak dresser with a looking glass, a pine table with a pitcher and basin and a book case over flowing with books. A large window with white, linen curtains faced the setting sun over the White Mountains of New Hampshire. He shook his head.

"Why did you decide to go to Ireland when it was not on your itinerary?" Joshua repeated the question in Darian's absence.

"When I was in Liverpool waiting to embark to New York I witnessed dilapidated ships filled with desperate Irish. They were escaping the Great Hunger by accepting free passage on ships from Dublin to Liverpool. There are anywhere from 250,000 to 300,000 of them crowded into cheap, unsanitary housing spreading typhus and other diseases. The city is so overrun with them that the authorities are beginning to ship them back to Ireland.[4] I knew there was a great story to pursue, so I left for Ireland."

"Why are hundreds of thousands of Irishmen leaving?" Hannah asked.

"The potato crop failed three out of four years in a row.[5] Entire families are starving."

"That is ridiculous. Why do they not eat turnips, or winter squash?" Benjamin contradicted. "They could go hunting or fishing. There is no reason for anyone to starve."

"You must understand the situation in Ireland. The vast majority are Catholic who supported Catholic Stuart King James II instead of Protestant William of Orange in 1690. Five years later the British passed the Penal Laws stripping Irish Catholics of the right to vote, to buy land, practice law, attend school, serve an apprenticeship or own weapons. The Catholic Church was outlawed and the Gaelic language was banned. Export trade was forbidden.[6] The Irish linen and woolen industries in the countryside collapsed because they could not compete with the English textile mills.[7]

As recently as five years ago, there were eight million Irish with seven million of them living in the rural countryside.[8] In 1798, Ireland, inspired by the American and French

Revolutions, staged a rebellion against the British. After the British quashed the rebellion they passed the British Act of Union in 1800. This made Ireland part of the United Kingdom and abolished the five-hundred-year-old independent Irish Parliament in Dublin. They were now to be represented by one hundred members to the British Parliament, but Catholics were to be excluded."[9]

"That is taxation without representation," Joshua observed grimly.

"The British landlord system is based on heredity with the ruling elite holding vast amounts of land. Many are absentee landlords living in England who only wish to extort the highest possible rents from their tenants with the least amount of improvements or reinvestment."[10]

"I understand that under the British rule, they had few options to improve their lot in life with no education, no professions, no voice in the government and no land holdings. What I do not understand is if the potato crop failed, why not eat something else?" his grandfather questioned.

"Potatoes are not native to Ireland. During the reign of Queen Elizabeth, Sir Walter Raleigh introduced the potato to Great Britain from the New World. They thrived in the mild and damp Irish climate, providing a good yield even on marginal lands. They gradually replaced grain as a staple for the poor."[11]

"Therefore, Ireland was overly dependent upon potatoes as their source of food. When the potato crop failed, they were left with nothing," Benjamin summarized the situation.

"Is that why you brought Darian home with you? His family could not afford to feed a growing boy?" Hannah asked with concern.

"There is no family. There is no one left," Thaddeus shook his head sadly. "In Liverpool I met a Quaker from the Central Relief Committee of the Society of Friends.[12] He told me of the mass starvation due to the potato blight. I volunteered to accompany him, to serve at the soup kitchens and to write a story for the New York Post."

"Are you telling us that potatoes are all those people ate?" Hannah asked in disbelief. Even in her poverty-stricken childhood in Virginia, people could find a variety of food in season.

"The poorest had the least amount of land to plant. One acre of potatoes could feed an entire family. In September of 1845 the potato leaves turned black, curled and rotted. The blight spread throughout the entire country side and one half of the crop perished due to wet rot.[13] They planted again in the summer of 46 and the plants appeared healthy until they succumbed to disease again. There were only enough potatoes to feed the Irish population for one month.[14]

Meanwhile the starving Irish watched boat loads of home grown oats and grains depart Irish ports for England. Food riots erupted when peasants tried to confiscate the boats of grain. British troops shot into the crowds.[15] Darian's father was there desperately trying to get food for his family. He never returned home. A neighbor told them that Mr. Flynn was shot and killed that day.

The winter of 46-47 brought bitter cold with one blizzard after another, burying houses in snow up to their roofs.[16] Darian's grandparents and baby sister died that winter.

That spring Darian's older brother sought employment on public works relief projects building stone roads to nowhere. I do not understand how the British could expect starving people dressed in rags to perform hard labor. Able bodied men were expected to work for their food. He, like thousands of others, collapsed from hunger and exhaustion and died on the side of the road.[17]

This past fall the potato harvest was blight free. Unfortunately only a quarter of the needed potatoes were planted last spring."

"Well, that was foolish. Why did they not plant more?" Benjamin asked in exasperation.

"The seed potatoes were eaten. Also most of the planters were already dead, too sick to work, homeless, in poor houses or employed in public works projects.[18] Unless you have witnessed their unmitigated suffering, no one should judge them. I arrived in Dublin where sick and starving hordes were clamoring to leave for Liverpool, America or Canada. A half a million Irish have been evicted from their little cottages for nonpayment. In desperation some of the landlords are paying to have these paupers transported to British North America.

These vessels are called coffin ships because they are overcrowded, filthy, poorly built and often not seaworthy. Many of the passengers are sick with typhus, spreading the disease to the healthy. Most of these ships head to Quebec where they are stopped at Grosse Isle in the St. Lawrence Sea Way to be inspected and quarantined. The dead are simply dumped in the river. The sick often die on the island unattended and without medical treatment. Last year Montreal received an influx of 100,000 Irish immigrants; twenty percent of whom died of disease and malnutrition.[19]

The soup kitchens never had enough food to feed the desperate crowds. The further west we traveled, the more desperate the situations. When our coach would stop for a meal, crowds of the famished poor flocked around begging for alms. A woman carrying the corpse of her child appealed to us passengers for aid to purchase a coffin and bury her child.[20] Every couple of hundred yards we would pass a funeral or a coffin.[21] The lucky ones had coffins.

We visited many hovels where mothers and their children lay dying. Many were widows whose husbands had recently been taken by the fever. Some were remnants of families crowded together in one cabin; the dead lying with the dying. The emaciated kin were too weak or sick to bury their dead. Many of the dead were buried without coffins a few inches below the soil, their bodies gnawed upon by starving rats and dogs.[22]

We found Darian attempting to dig a shallow grave for his younger brother who had died two days previously. He was unaware that his mother too had recently expired. We promised if Darian came with us, we would see that his family received a Christian burial in the local Catholic cemetery.

We fed, bathed and clothed him. It took two weeks before he spoke a word to us. We planned to take him to a local work house. Unfortunately, many people seeking refuge were refused admission due to overcrowding.[23] Women with six or seven starving children would beg the work house to take even two or three of them. Two thirds of the inmates are children; most of them are orphans.[24] I simply could not leave him there."

"I only wish you had brought more children home with you," Hannah solemnly stated. "Our home will always be a refuge for those in need. To whom much have been given, much will be required."

Darian had never slept in his own bed before; his family always slept in one room. As he nestled between the linen sheets he thought, "America is a wonderful place! The houses are big, there is plenty of food cooking on iron boxes and everyone sleeps in his own bed."

III

Saturday on the Farm

Benjamin, Hannah, Joshua and Abigail were eating breakfast when a disheveled and barefoot Thaddeus entered the kitchen. Joshua shot his son a disapproving glare.

"In this family we appear for meals properly dressed and groomed," Hannah sternly reminded him.

"I am hungry," he shrugged.

"That is no way to address your grandmother," Joshua reprimanded.

"Please, Joshua, let us enjoy our breakfast together. He will get washed and dressed later," Abigail interrupted.

The kitchen door opened and then slammed. "Grandpa, can I come live with you? I can sleep in…" Isaac stopped short when he saw Thaddeus seated at the table. "We thought you were dead."

"I am sorry to disappoint you," Thaddeus smirked.

"I am very pleased to see you are alive. I just wanted to move into your bedroom," he explained.

"Is Eli bossing you around again?" Joshua asked sympathetically for he grew up with six older brothers.

"Julia brought the children to spend the day while she helps Mama with the baking. Becky is churning butter, Victoria is sewing with Aunt Grace and Davy wants me to play with him all day," he rolled his eyes.

"There is nothing worse than being forced to play with your youngest cousin!" Thaddeus laughed.

Isaac ignored the insult. "Davy is not my cousin. He is my nephew," he corrected. "Who is that?" he pointed to Darian who had washed, brushed his hair and put on the wool tweed outfit which he had worn yesterday.

"This is our guest, Darian Flynn from Ireland," Hannah introduced. "Perhaps you would like to spend the day showing Darian the farm?"

"Dressed like that?" Isaac asked incredulously.

"Come with me upstairs, I am sure we could find some of Thaddeus' old clothes more suitable to outdoor play," Hannah invited. Darian followed Hannah and Isaac upstairs to the spare bedroom which was crammed with old furniture and half dozen wooden trunks filled with clothing. The third trunk they opened held several pairs of trousers, two linen shirts, two vests, a straw hat, cotton stockings with garters and old pair of leather shoes. "Perfect," she smiled as she handed the clothing to Darian.

"For me?" he asked in astonishment. He had never owned so many clothes in his life.

"It is a sin to keep these in a trunk when others have need of them. Run along and get dressed. After breakfast I need you two boys to help me carry my rag basket to the farm. Time is wasting."

The boys walked slowly down the lane so Hannah would not be left behind. Darian quietly took it all in – the large two-story, white house attached to a larger red barn, acres of newly planted fields by the winding Saco River and a covered bridge. Across the river was a small house, more fields and trees. Beyond the trees were mountains. Above the mountains were sapphire blue skies with white puffy clouds. "America is a beautiful country," he thought.

Jacob greeted them in the front yard, "It is a glorious morning!"

"Thaddeus is not dead. He came home last night," Isaac informed his father.

"That is certainly an answer to our prayers. My sister must be relieved," he said as he took the rag basket.

"We all are," Hannah added. "Jacob, this is Darian and he is visiting from Ireland. Darian, this is my son and Isaac's father, Jacob Miller."

Darian observed the three of them with their soft gray eyes, kind smile and curly hair – black, gray and white. The boy tentatively shook Jacob's out stretched hand.

"I am going to show him the farm. We should go in the barn because the house is filled with girls," Isaac warned.

Hannah found her great granddaughter, Victoria, sitting in the front room with Grace. Grace was cutting wool scraps into strips while the eight-year-old, curly-haired girl was sewing a dress for her porcelain doll. "I have some worn out, wool pants and scraps from an old brown great coat. When we are done cutting these down, I am sure there will be enough for a rug."

Jacob's wife, Kate, entered and turned to her granddaughter, "Victoria I need you to churn some butter. You can sew your little dress later."

"Kate, Fryeburg needs seamstresses as much as milk maids. Leave us be. You have Julia, Rachel and Becky helping you," Grace scolded.

Kate bit her tongue and wordlessly returned to the kitchen. "Grace, Thaddeus returned home last night. He spent six weeks in Ireland and brought home an orphan. Let me tell Kate the good news before I begin here."

Hannah entered the busy kitchen. "Good morning, Nana," her twenty-eight-year-old granddaughter, Rachel, stopped her churning long enough to kiss her on the cheek. "Are you spending the day with us?"

"Most of it. I have come to tell you the good news that Thaddeus returned last night."

"I am sure Abigail and Joshua are relieved. I am thankful that my children had the good sense to stay in Fryeburg." Kate and Jacob had four children: the eldest son Elijah and his wife Julia built a new house just over the river where they lived with their three children. Eli was here every day working the farm with his father. Julia helped her mother-in-law twice a week on baking days.

Rachel lived at home working in the family creamery, helping her mother run the house and caring for Isaac. Of course Isaac would be living at home for several more years. Their second son, Daniel, and his wife, Emily, did not live nearby although they still lived in Fryeburg.

"I am thankful for that as well," Hannah smiled. "I am also thankful that my son married such a talented and hard working woman. Grace and Sadie could not possibly run this house alone if you and Jacob were not living here as well. Thank you for understanding that Victoria is doing more than sewing doll clothes. She is keeping Grace entertained during this difficult time. Becky, you are a big help to your grandmother. Now if you will excuse me, I have wool scraps to cut."

"I have plenty of beans baking in the oven. Please invite the family over for supper. We will celebrate Thaddeus' homecoming," Kate called after her mother-in-law.

Darian surveyed the neat and orderly barn. Two of the largest horses he had ever seen tilted their heads and stared at him as if to ask, "Do we know you?" He took a step back.

"Do not be afraid. They may be big, but they are gentle," Isaac reassured.

Darian could see the other two horses pulling a plow in the field closest to the river. The sheep pen held a couple of ewes and lambs; the rest of the flock was grazing outside. Four Jersey cows, the source of Kate's creamery business, were also outside grazing. One wall was neatly lined with saws and wood working tools. Darian looked up to the large hayloft above. In America even the animals had better houses than the Irish did back home.

"Isaac, I was looking all over for you," four-year-old David Miller whined. "Do you want to play checkers?"

"Davy, not now!" Isaac rolled his eyes in exasperation.

Undeterred, Davy turned to Darian, "Do you want to play checkers?"

"I do not know how," he stammered.

"I can teach you. Come on!" he ran to the side yard where a checker board was set up on a tree stump.

"Have fun!" Isaac laughed as he left the two boys and headed out to the field to his father.

"Where have you been?" Eli demanded as Isaac approached. Why is it you are never around when it is time to work, but you are always around when it is time to eat?"

"You are not my father! You are just my brother and I do not have to tell you where I have been," Isaac retorted.

Jacob intervened, "Isaac was helping his grandmother. Thaddeus has returned home and has brought a young friend from Ireland with him. Isaac will spend the day being a good host. Elijah, there is plenty of other work for this family to do like bringing in the water bucket or the firewood, helping mother with deliveries, carrying things for Aunt Grace and Nana. I remember a certain ten-year-old who loved working outdoors in the field, but was rather remiss in his other obligations. I also seem to remember you bribing, blackmailing or bullying Daniel into doing some of your chores."

Isaac stifled a giggle. "Spoiled," Eli mumbled under his breath. Jacob winked at his youngest son.

Davy and Darian entered the kitchen. "I taught Darian to play checkers and he won," Davy announced. "I am going to show him how to play pick-up sticks."

"You must be the Irish boy," Kate greeted. "I am Mrs. Miller, Isaac's mother." She carefully took loaves of wheat bread out of the oven. "This is my daughter, Rachel, my daughter-in-law, Julia and granddaughter Becky." They were packing the freshly churned butter into molds.

Darian looked around at the kitchen in amazement. Ten years ago, Jacob had built a large extension to the kitchen. In addition to the original field stone hearth and a long, pine trestle table, there was a large cook stove. To the left was a walk- in pantry with shelves lined with salt glazed stoneware. He could only guess the contents. To the right was the buttery where Kate stored her milk pans, butter churns, butter molds, cheese cloth. A flight of steps led to a small root cellar where food was kept cool in the summer and protected from freezing in the winters.

"We will have dinner within the hour. I fear it will not be anything fancy – just salt pork, dandelion greens, and bread and butter."

"America is a wonderful place. People eat three meals a day," Darian thought. He studied the family gathered around the pine table.

"Let me make this simple for you, Darian. If it is a man, he is Mr. Miller, a married woman Mrs. Miller and a girl Miss Miller." Isaac explained.

Darian silently nodded. He once had grandparents, parents and siblings he thought bitterly. Now he had no one. He listened to their chatter, laughter and bickering. Everyone had responsibilities and a purpose. Darian had none. He had nothing except some borrowed clothing and the food in his stomach.

"Kate, perhaps Julia and Davy would like to accompany you to the general store today. This will give Rachel and the girls the opportunity to prepare tonight's meal, giving you a few moments to yourself this afternoon. I will escort my mother home. I am sure Davy would enjoy the outing while Isaac spends some time with our guest," Jacob winked at his youngest son.

Isaac flashed a smile of gratitude to his father as Davy excitedly squealed. He was free for an entire afternoon – no school, no Davy and no Eli telling him what to do!

"Thaddeus, you have only just arrived! How can you think about leaving next week?" Abigail beseeched.

"Mother, please do not make a scene. I have a job to do."

"What about the boy?" Joshua asked.

"I was hoping he could stay here with you."

Benjamin and Hannah looked at one another before Benjamin spoke, "This home has been a haven for all who were seeking safety and freedom. The lad may stay for as long as he wishes."

"Please allow me to invite him," Hannah suggested. "We cannot demand that he stay here."

"What is so important that you cannot stay home for one more week?" Abigail demanded.

"The Democratic Convention will be meeting on May 22 in Baltimore. President Polk promised to be a one-term President and this leaves the field wide open.[1] Then I leave for Philadelphia for the Whigs National Convention on June 7.[2] Later I set sail from Philadelphia for England."

"Why are you returning to Europe so soon?" Abigail asked in exasperation.

"I have an interview with Karl Marx next month."

"I have never heard of him," Joshua said.

"No. But some day the whole world will."

It was a pleasant and breezy evening when Joshua hitched the horses to the carriage. "Shall we not walk? It is a beautiful evening." Thaddeus questioned.

"I fear even the short walk to the farm is too much for your grandfather. He has had a few falls this past year and Nana insists he take the carriage."

"Well, I shall meet you there," Thaddeus strolled out of the stable.

Saturday on the Farm

Eli greeted his cousin as Thaddeus entered the front yard. "Welcome home, Thad. It is good to see you." Eli shook his hand and slapped him on the back with the other. "It has been over two years. Let me show you Weston's Covered Bridge. Danny cut the lumber for it. Have you seen his mill?"

Thaddeus shook his head. "I only arrived last evening."

"Well, he has expanded the operation. As you can see, we have expanded the farm as well. Is not this bridge a beauty? That is my house over there," he pointed across the river with pride. "Last week we tilled five new acres."

"The bridge is very nice. But if you wish to see a real bridge, you should see the new London Bridge they built in '31. It is over 900 feet long and almost 50 feet wide and constructed from granite.[3]

Eli whistled, "That is one big bridge. I hear London is a dirty, crowded city. I could never live in a place like that."

"Some parts are dirty," Thaddeus conceded. "But you should see Buckingham Palace!"

"Has Queen Victoria invited you to tea?" Eli teased. At the sound of the carriage's arrival, he headed to his grandfather. "Grandpa, please allow me to help you down."

"I have missed you, Elijah. I understand that a farmer does not have time to socialize in planting season. That is why I thoroughly enjoyed your frequent visits this winter."

"Not as much as I have enjoyed them, sir. May we have many more visits next winter." The rugged farmer gently helped his frail grandfather to the ground, before offering a hand to his grandmother.

Isaac and Darian came running across the field. "Grandpa, we found the beaver lodge," he panted. "Darian said America has the biggest rats he ever saw!"

Darian scowled as everyone laughed.

"Isaac, beavers do not live in Ireland. Darian would not have had the opportunity to see one before." Benjamin defended his young guest. "Darian, perhaps you would like to see some moose, or raccoons or woodchucks as well. There is plenty of wildlife in Maine."

"I can teach you how to identify animal tracks," Isaac offered.

"America is a very big country with very strange animals," the Irish boy observed.

"You boys must be hungry. Run in the house and wash up for supper," Hannah suggested as she took Benjamin's arm and headed up the steps.

To Darian's surprise the family gathered in another room, around another table and ate off of another set of dishes. Americans had a special room just for eating!

"Where is Uncle Micah?" Thaddeus innocently asked.

The room fell silent. "Uncle Micah passed away two months ago," Abigail quietly explained.

"Aunt Grace, I am so sorry! I have the fondest memories of Uncle Micah taking me to tap maple trees and making maple sugar."

"The entire town turned out for his funeral," Sadie added with pride.

"They do not make men like Uncle Micah anymore," Eli commented. "He was a hard working farmer right until the day he died."

"We have suffered a big loss," Benjamin swallowed the lump in his throat as he patted Grace's hand.

Darian sat there in icy silence. These people knew nothing about suffering loss.

Eli abruptly changed the subject. "Thaddeus, have you seen the new church we are building? Fryeburg is growing by leaps and bounds."

"You have not seen a church until you have visited Notre Dame Cathedral in Paris," Thaddeus replied.

"I think flying buttresses would look rather silly on Main Street," Grace laughed.

"Sadie, you should come to Paris with me someday and visit the Louvre," Thaddeus invited.

Sadie looked confused. "What is this Louvre?"

"It is a museum filled with masterpieces from all over the world. Every artist should visit the Louvre at least once in a lifetime," he explained.

"Perhaps I shall one day. Thank you for supper, Kate. If you excuse me I am in the middle of painting. It is good to see you again, Thaddeus." She stood up and left the room.

Kate bit her tongue. Sadie never helped with the cooking and the cleaning. She knew it was useless to complain to her husband who always defended his cousin. "We are enjoying the fruits of Aunt Grace's and Sadie's wealth. Where do you think the money for the cook stove, the new pantry and creamery came from? Sadie financially supports this family. Someday this house, the furnishings and the farm will be ours. Is it really that difficult to cook for two extra people and to wash two extra plates?" he would admonish.

"Where is Danny?" Thaddeus asked.

"He is extremely busy cutting lumber for Walker's bridge," Jacob explained. You will see him tomorrow at church."

"He and Emily have Sunday dinner with us each week," Hannah added. She noticed her husband's fatigue. "I thank you for a lovely meal, Kate."

"It is only pork and beans," Kate replied modestly.

"Yes, but I thank you for your thoughtfulness in inviting us together to celebrate Thaddeus' arrival. I fear the excitement of the past twenty-four hours have worn us out."

"First a concert, then home," Benjamin contradicted. Fifteen years ago, he had surprised everyone with the purchase of a piano from Chickering and Company in Boston. "Rachel, please play Chopin."

She began Nocturne in C-sharp minor. "I could listen to you play all evening," Benjamin sighed.

"Rachel, you play almost as well as Chopin himself," Thaddeus complimented.

Rachel stopped playing and stared at her cousin. "You have met Chopin?"

"Not personally but I attended his concert in February at the Salle Pleyel in Paris. Please continue."

At the conclusion of the recital Joshua offered, "Sir, let me drive the two of you home. I have work waiting for me in the office. I know Abigail would enjoy staying to visit. Thaddeus, please escort your mother home when she is ready to leave."

Thaddeus was not accustomed to having other people tell him what to do. A knowing glance from his grandmother prompted him to reply, "Yes, sir."

Darian stifled a yawn. "You have had an exhausting journey and a busy day. Growing boys need their rest. Would you like to come home with us?" Hannah invited. "It will be a very busy day tomorrow."

IV

Keeping the Sabbath

"What do you mean you will not be attending church?" Joshua demanded at breakfast.

"I have grown out of the habit," Thaddeus replied.

"Worshipping the Almighty is not a habit. It is a command. If you are living under my roof, you will abide by my rules."

"This is not your house, is it? It is Grandpa's" he flippantly retorted.

"Yes and I say get dressed and get in the carriage," Benjamin answered crossly. "Your forefathers suffered great persecution for their faith. I will not allow any grandchild of mine to scoff at their sacrifice."

He rarely saw his grandfather angry. "Yes, sir."

Darian stayed up half the night worrying about what he was going to say. "Sir, I am an Irishman. My conscience will not allow me to attend an English Church. My family, my people have been persecuted for our faith as well." He tried his best to imitate Thaddeus.

Benjamin cast a dirty look to Thaddeus who innocently shrugged. "We are not attending a British Church, we are attending an American Church," Benjamin patiently explained.

"The Lord's Church knows no borders. He is not restricted to nationalities," Hannah corrected.

"I believe what our guest is saying, as a persecuted Catholic he does not wish to attend a Protestant Church," Joshua explained.

"Yes, sir," Darian smiled at Joshua in gratitude.

"He and I shall keep the Sabbath together at home," Hannah announced. "Perhaps you would be kind enough to explain the tenets of your faith to me. All of you run along. Darian, if you could carry my cup of tea outside, we shall sit in the shade and talk.

Please pardon my ignorance for I am not a scholar like my husband," Hannah apologized. "I was illiterate until my twenties when Mr. Miller taught me to read. I know very little about Ireland and your faith. Perhaps you could enlighten me."

Darian was speechless for he had never met anyone like this kind, elderly woman. "Well Ireland is a beautiful island. It is not as big as America, but it is just as beautiful. Before St. Patrick came, the Irish were pagans"

"Who is Saint Patrick?"

"You never heard of St. Patrick?" Darian asked in amazement. He had memorized the story of St. Patrick that his parish priest told him years ago. "A long time ago St. Patrick was born in Britain to a Roman family. When he was sixteen years old, he was captured by Irish pirates, brought to Ireland and sold into slavery."

"He was a slave? What happened to him?" she asked eagerly.

"His master was a Druid, a pagan, and his job was to tend the sheep."

"He was a shepherd just like David in the Bible," she added.

"When he was a slave he became very religious and prayed constantly."

"How did he become a Christian if he was a Roman?"

"My priest told me that by the 4th century Romans were Christians and Christianity had spread as far north as Britain."

"But not to Ireland?"

"Not yet. In a vision he saw the children of pagan Ireland reaching out their hands to him. But he escaped his master and convinced some sailors to let him board their ship and he returned to England."

"That was good that Patrick was able to return home. His parents must have been worried. What happened next?"

"He went to France to study for the priesthood. The Pope consecrated him to be the Bishop of the Irish and sent him to Ireland to spread the Gospel to the pagans."

"He went back to his captors!" she gasped. Hannah remembered her childhood as a slave on a plantation in Virginia. As the illegitimate child of her white master and a light skinned slave, she was despised by both her black and white families. After her father's death at Valley Forge, she was sold to a Quaker couple and raised in Philadelphia. It was only her light complexion and her husband's love which led to her comfortable life and freedom. Of course this was all a secret. She often wondered if she would be accepted by the good people of Fryeburg if they knew of her heritage. She would never jeopardize her freedom to return to the plantation to preach the gospel. Yet that is exactly what this man Patrick did.

"He spent the rest of his life preaching, writing and performing countless baptism. He convinced the Druids that they were worshiping idols. That is how Ireland became Christian."[1]

"You know your history very well. Did you learn it in school?"

"I have never been to school. My priest taught me everything I know about history. Everything was fine until Henry VIII," He said bitterly.

"I know this story!" Hannah interrupted. "England was a Catholic country until Henry VIII wanted to divorce his wife, Catherine of Aragon, because there was no male heir. When the Pope refused to grant the divorce King Henry renounced

England's attachment to Rome, established the Church of England and made himself the head of the Church.[2] Mr. Miller told me this story hundreds of times."

"A king cannot be a pope!" Darian added. "Many Catholics had to run for their lives."

"England was Protestant until Henry died and his Catholic daughter, Mary, the daughter of Catherine of Aragon became queen. Henry had many wives you know. Some he divorced and some he killed. What a despicable man! His daughter was not much better because she executed many Protestants and many had to flee for their lives."

"I never heard that story before," Darian admitted. "What happened?"

"She even imprisoned her half-sister Elizabeth because she was Protestant and the Protestants wanted her to be Queen. When Mary died, Elizabeth did become Queen and ruled for a long time.

Then there was a group of Christians who wanted to purify the Church of England. As a result they were persecuted for their beliefs. A small group escaped to Holland and then to the New World on a ship called the Mayflower and settled in Plymouth. Mr. Miller's ancestor, William Bradford was one of those Pilgrims.

As fear and discontent with King Charles grew, a larger group of Puritans left for America. They wanted the freedom to exercise their faith without the tyranny of King Charles and the Church of England.[3]

I understand your anger at the British. But this is America. No one will force you to go to a certain church."

"Mr. Miller forced Thaddeus to go to church," Darian observed.

Hannah laughed. "I stand corrected. The government cannot force you to attend a particular church. Grandfathers are a different story."

"I want to return to Ireland and fight the British," he said defiantly.

"I understand. My father fought the British in the American Revolution and served under General Washington. Mr. Miller's uncle fought the British at the Battle of Lexington. We were only children then and did not really understand the events of the day."

"I will fight the British as well," Darian repeated.

"May I suggest that you grow up first and learn how to shoot a gun?" she smiled. "I was an orphan too. My father died of smallpox and my mother was too poor to take care of me. An elderly couple took me in and raised me until I married Mr. Miller. Darian, Thaddeus plans to leave Fryeburg next week to travel for the newspaper. Mr. Miller and I would like you to stay with us for a few years. We want you to be like a grandson."

"Like Isaac?"

"Yes, like Isaac. You would have Thaddeus' bedroom for yourself and all the food a growing boy can eat. There will be no need to steal bread. Do you know the Ten Commandments? The eighth commandment says 'Thou shalt not steal'."

"I have never stolen any bread," the boy lied.

"The next commandment is 'Thou shalt not bear false witness'. Would your St. Patrick steal and then lie about it?" she questioned.

"No, mam," he hung his head in shame.

"When I was a child I often went hungry. I confess that I have stolen some food myself. As long as you are living in this house, you will never go hungry. If you would like some bread and butter at bed time, please ask. There is no need to steal."

"Yes, mam."

"You will go to school, learn a trade, learn to hunt and to grow crops. Then when you are a man, you are free to return to Ireland if you choose."

"Mr. Miller will not force me to go to church?" he eyed her suspiciously.

"You leave Mr. Miller to me," she patted him on the arm as the carriage returned.

Darian ran to help Benjamin down just as Eli had done the night before.

"We have enjoyed a wonderful Sabbath. Darian taught me about St. Patrick."

"Mrs. Miller taught me about the Pilgrims," he added.

"I shall lend you a copy of *The Confessions of St. Patrick*. I have it somewhere in my office."

By the look of panic on Darian's face, Hannah surmised that he could not read. "We shall read it together on Sundays."

"I decided to stay in Fryeburg until I am ready to return to Ireland and fight the British," he proudly announced.

A glum looking Thaddeus silently entered the house as a horse and wagon arrived.

"This is the last of the grandchildren, Daniel Miller and his wife Emily. You have now met all of us. Danny and Emily attend Sunday dinners with us," Hannah introduced as the couple entered the yard.

"Darian, it is indeed a pleasure to meet you. Could you help me unhitch the horses?"

He hesitated and then quietly confided, "I have never handled a horse before."

"Then you shall learn something new today." Darian thought Daniel smiled just like his grandmother.

The family gathered around the dining room table and said grace. No one commented when Darian made the sign of the cross. Hannah made a mental note to ask him about that when they were in private.

"Thaddeus, where have you been?" Daniel asked politely.

"I have been traveling throughout Europe, England and Ireland. After the political conventions I will return to England with hopes of interviewing Karl Marx."

"Who?"

"Karl Marx is a revolutionary who will change the world."

"Thaddeus, the big story is right here in America. The country is splitting into two over slavery," Daniel pointed out.

"You speak of treason, cousin."

"I speak the truth. You have been out of the country too long. Look at the churches. The Methodist Church with a million members has split – 15,000 abolitionists left. The remaining split in half into the proslavery Methodist Episcopal Church, South and the anti-slavery faction called the Methodist Episcopal Church. Three years ago the Baptists split into two independent wings. The Presbyterians split into the Old School South and the New School North.[4]

Look at what is happening to the two political parties. The Democrats have split into the Abolitionists who call themselves Barn Burners and the proslavery Hunkers. The Whig Party has divided into the Conscience Whigs who are abolitionists and the Mainline Whigs.[5]

I am surprised that you are not reporting on the annexation of Texas. Can you imagine the repercussions if Texas enters as a slave state?"

"I was unaware that you took such an interest in politics. I thought that was Eli's domain and you were the religious one," Thaddeus stated coolly.

"We are grandsons of a Quaker," Daniel nodded to Hannah, "with a rich heritage of oppositions to slavery. William Wilberforce was a man of great faith and he eradicated slavery from the entire British Empire fifteen years ago.[6] This is not a matter of politics; it is a matter of faith. Charles Finney says, 'Slavery is a blatant violation of God's command to love thy neighbor.' Slavery is simply immoral and against God's principles."[7]

"So you use the Bible to condemn slavery and the South uses the Bible to defend it. What side is God on?" Thaddeus challenge.

Abigail intervened, "Let us not spoil our only Sunday dinner together quarreling about politics."

"I am sorry, Aunt Abigail. I have been a poor guest," Daniel apologized. "Darian, perhaps you would like to come out and visit my lumber mill sometime. I could teach you how to saw wood."

Darian decided that next to Hannah, Daniel was his favorite Miller. He was going to learn to read, to farm and hunt and now learn to saw wood. He was allowed to adhere to his Catholic faith. America was a land of freedom and opportunities.

V

Journey to Buffalo

During the next two months, Darian grew two inches and gained ten pounds; his light brown hair was bleached flaxen by the summer sun. After his morning chores, he and Hannah spent two hours reading and writing.

Benjamin had purchased a new set of *McGuffey's Eclectic Readers Primer through the Sixth*. Hannah opened to the first page of the primer. "This is the alphabet in capital letters and this is the alphabet in lower case. Each letter has a name and makes a sound. This week we will learn this and we will write them in our copy book. When we put these letters together, we will make words."

Reading was a mystery to Darian and yet Hannah made it sound so simple.

"In lesson one, all we need to know are the letters a, e, d, n, r and t. Now put these letters with their sounds together."

An hour later Darian haltingly read, "*A cat and a rat. A rat and a cat.*" He laughed with joy because he was actually reading.

"Now write that sentence in your copy book ten times."

He dipped one of Benjamin's quills into the ink pot and began capital A when a large drop of ink fell on the page. He accidentally smeared it with his cuff. He felt like flinging the book across the room in anger.

"May I suggest that we roll up our sleeves? I found learning to write to be more challenging than learning to read," she admitted. "Blots and smears are part of learning. If you practice an hour each day I promise you that within a few months you shall see improvement."

Two weeks later he was reading Lesson VIII, "*See the lamp! It is on a mat. The mat is on the stand. The lamp is Nat's, and the mat is Ann's.*"

Hannah had borrowed Isaac's slate for the summer. "This will save paper, ink and shirt sleeves," she smiled.

"What are the letters in my name?" he asked.

Hannah printed his name on the slate. Slowly and carefully he copied each letter. If only his mother could see him now!

"You are making rapid progress," Hannah complimented.

"I have a good teacher."

"Well I have had years of experience. When Mr. Miller and I were living in Washington City, I opened a school for freed blacks," she explained.

After his studies he would help Isaac with his chores on the farm and play with Davy. Benjamin and Hannah alternated the weeks keeping the Sabbath with Darian.

One morning at breakfast Joshua entered the kitchen, "Sir, this letter from John Quincy Adams arrived. I thought perhaps it may be important."

Benjamin carefully tore the wax seal and quickly scanned the letter. "Joshua, please ride out to the mill and ask Daniel to come right away," he instructed.

"Grandpa?" Daniel entered the front parlor.

"Please take a seat. I received a letter from John Quincy Adams this morning." The two men had been friends since 1825 when Mr. Adams served his only term as President and Benjamin served his first term as United States Senator. "The abolitionists have decided to hold a convention in Buffalo, New York where they plan to form a new political party."

"That is astounding!"

"Yes and Mr. Adams invited me to serve as one of the 450 delegates."

"Congratulations, sir. What a way to culminate your political career!"

Benjamin sadly shook his head. "I am no longer a young man. I cannot attend. That is why I wish you to attend in my stead."

"Why me? Sir, I have never left the town of Fryeburg, I could not travel to Buffalo," he argued.

"You have been to New Hampshire."

"I have been to East Conway, one half mile over the bridge," Daniel corrected.

"I will pay all expenses for you and Emily. Do you remember that Aunt Grace's son, Alden, lives in Buffalo? I ask that you two escort Grace and Sadie to Boston to meet with her daughter Libby. Then the five of you will travel together. Grace and Libby are familiar in traveling the Erie Canal for they have visited Buffalo several times. I believe this is a good time for Aunt Grace to spend some time with her children."

"Why me? Why not Eli? He enjoys politics." Eli was presently a Fryeburg selectman.

"There are two good reasons. First, you know a farmer cannot leave his farm at the height of haying season. Emily's brother can supervise the mill in your absence. Secondly, you have the passion of an abolitionist. You remind me of your grandmother."

After three days of flurried activity, Daniel, Emily, Sadie and Grace loaded their trunks unto the back of the wagon. "Aunt Grace, you are staying a month, not a year," Joshua teased.

Grace laughed good naturedly with a twinkle in her eyes. Daniel had to admit that this trip did brighten Aunt Grace's and Sadie's demeanor. Joshua headed the carriage down the

Main Street, turned right onto the Pequawket Trail to Portland. They would take a ship to Boston where they would spend a few days before embarking to New York City.

"I have received a most disturbing letter from Grace," Hannah confided to her husband in the privacy of his office two weeks later.

Dear family,
The Irish have over run the city of Boston like vermin! Libby says there are 37,000 of them huddled together in crowded, unsanitary housing. It is not safe for a lady to leave her home for crime and disease has increased dramatically. Thousands of children dressed in rags roam the streets begging.

My grandfather's beautiful three story home on the water front has a hundred Irish living in it. People are living in the gardens, yards and alleys.[1]

Edward and Libby have decided to sell the ship building business that has been in our family for four generations and move to Buffalo. What has happened to the beautiful city of my childhood?

Two weeks later another letter arrived posted from Rochester, New York.

Dear Grandpa and Nana,
I thought I would update you on our travels. Boston and New York were crowded, dirty and noisy. I had wished I had stayed home in Fryeburg! The trip up the Hudson River was simply beautiful. Sadie pulled out her easel and painted. Soon she had quite an audience watching her paint. Traveling on a steamboat made me uneasy. Emily was convinced the ship would blow up any minute.

The Erie Canal is a wonder to behold! First I prefer the canal boats with the donkeys traveling on tow paths pulling the boat along. Occasionally one must duck under a bridge. The boat actually goes uphill! A gate opens and then closes behind you. A gate in front of you opens and lets water pour in until the boat is lifted up. You can feel the boat rising under you.

Aunt Grace, Libby and Sadie spend their days telling us stories from "the old days". I never knew Aunt Grace could be so funny! Grandpa, she had a few tales to tell about you! It is good to see the three of them talking and laughing like school girls.

I will be glad to be standing on solid ground once again.
Your devoted grandson,
Daniel

Alden Miller greeted the family as they arrived in the bustling city of Buffalo on August 7. Daniel quietly stood aside and watched the hugs and tears between mother and son, brother and sisters. "Mother, I am so sorry I could not be there," Alden repeated.

"The important thing is we are together now," Grace wiped her tears and smiled. "Where are my manners? Alden this is Jacob's second son, Daniel, and his wife, Emily."

Daniel shook the outstretched hand. "I am pleased to meet you sir. I am so sorry for your loss. Uncle Micah was like a second grandfather to me since we children grew up on the farm."

"It is a comfort to me knowing that my father was surrounded by his family." He smiled at his mother before changing the subject. "My dear wife has been cooking for a week and I have strict instructions to bring everyone straight home. Daniel, I will show you around town once we get the ladies settled."

Lake Erie appeared as big as an ocean to Daniel. He had never seen so many ships in his life.

"Tens of thousands of travelers come to the port of Buffalo to head west," Alden explained. "Our future is to the west.

The harbor has expanded several times to keep up with the demand of shipping grains and commercial goods. Five years ago we built the world's first steam powered grain elevator. This enables faster unloading of lake freighters and transshipment of grain in bulk from lakers to canal boats."[2]

"My grandfather says you are a business man like your Grandfather Peabody."

Alden laughed. "That is the only explanation for how a farm boy from Fryeburg grew up to be a ship builder and merchant in Buffalo."

Daniel tried not to stare at all the Negroes freely walking down the street. "This is Macedonia Baptist Church. It is a Negro church and a meeting place for us abolitionists. It is easy for the fugitive slaves to mingle out in the open before they cross the Niagara River to Fort Erie, Ontario. It is much easier to transport runaways here than at your saw mill in Fryeburg."

Daniel stopped in his tracks. Alden patted him on the back, "When we were ten or twelve years old your father and I escorted a few visitors down the Saco. I understand you have taken over the family avocation." Alden sensed his discomfort. "People tell me there is anywhere between 10,000 and 20,000 abolitionists converging in Buffalo this week. Your secret is safe here." They turned into a tavern. "There is someone who would like to meet you."

"Alden, my friend," a distinguished middle aged man in a black suit rose to greet them.

"Charles, this is Senator Benjamin Miller's grandson, Daniel Miller, from Fryeburg, Maine. Daniel, this is Charles Francis Adams, a leader in the abolitionist movement."

"The Miller and Adams families have been friends for generations. Your great grandmother, Sarah and my grandmother Abigail were friends from childhood. Your grandfather and my father became good friends when they were serving in Washington City."

"Sir, you are the son of President John Quincy Adams? My grandfather says President Adams has done more for the abolitionist movement as a member of the House of Representatives from Massachusetts than any president ever could. It is truly an honor, sir."

"Would you like ale?" Mr. Adams offered. Daniel shook his head as Alden explained, "His grandmother is a Quaker, an abolitionist and a member of the Temperance Society in Maine."

Mr. Adams whistled. "And I thought I had much to live up to!" he laughed. "It has been an upward battle. You must understand that we abolitionists are a minority, even in the North. The South has grown increasingly more hostile to the criticism against expanding slavery.[3] Initially we tried to convince the South that slavery was immoral and against God's principles. The South threatened to lynch anyone caught carrying abolitionist literature.[4] A vigilance committee in Columbia, South Carolina offered a reward of $1,500 to anyone who gives information identifying a distributor of *The Liberator,* an abolitionist's newspaper printed in Boston.[5] We tried mailing our literature until Southern Congressmen persuaded President Andrew Jackson to ban abolitionist literature in the U.S. mail."

"What do you expect from a southern President?" Alden added. What Alden did not mention it was President Jackson who defeated President John Quincy Adams in the 1828 election.

"We petitioned Congress to ban slavery in the District of Columbia. In response, proslavery congressmen passed a Gag Rule stipulating that any petition on the subject of slavery would be tabled and neither read nor discussed at all.

We have flooded Congress with hundreds and hundreds of petitions year after year. The harder the proslavery forces work to squelch our petitions, the more zealously we work to circulate them and the more northerners joined our cause.[6] Seven northern states passed laws stipulating that no state personnel or facilities are to be used in aiding the capture or return of any fugitive slaves. If the federal government is determined to drag people away into slavery, they will have to provide for the matter on their own. Unfortunately the Supreme Court decided that all state legislation on this matter is unconstitutional,"[7] Charles Adams lamented.

"The Supreme Court should be more concerned about being moral than being popular," Alden shook his head with disgust.

"My grandfather says someday there will be a civil war," Daniel stated. "I fear he may be right."

"I pray that he may be wrong," Charles Adams replied.

Official sessions of the convention met in a large church while abolitionist speakers addressed huge crowds in the city park. The 450 delegates from all of the Free States, the District of Columbia and three of the Border States worked to form a new antislavery coalition.[8] The platform called for a thorough separation of the federal government from the institution of slavery. While admitting a lack of constitutional authority to end slavery in the states where it already exists, the platform stipulated the federal government should ban slavery in every place where federal authority did prevail including all of the western territories.

Joshua Leavitt, a Congregationalist minister from Ohio concluded, "Free Soil, Free, Speech, Free Labor and Free Men."[9] Daniel with the other delegates in the church rose to his feet cheering. They named their party the Free Soil Party and nominated Martin Van Buren for President and Charles Francis Adams for Vice-President.[10] This was a day the humble sawyer from Fryeburg would never forget.

VI

Karl Marx

Thaddeus nervously approached a nondescript flat in a working class London neighborhood and knocked on the front door. "Please inform Mr. Marx that Thaddeus Pierce, from the New York Post has arrived."

A dour-looking, middle aged woman silently let Thaddeus in and led him to a cramped study. Marx looked up from his papers, "They sent me a boy," he mumbled to himself in German.

"Sir, I am wiser than my years," he replied in German.

"And you have read my manifesto?" Marx asked in English.

"Indeed I have. I am fluent in German, French, Latin, Greek and Hebrew. Would you prefer to conduct your interview in German?"

"English will be fine," he scowled behind his bushy beard.

"What inspired you to write the *Communist Manifesto?*"

"The history of all hitherto existing society is the history of class struggles – freeman and slave, patrician and plebian, lord and serf, guild master and journeyman–in a word the oppressor and the oppressed.

The modern bourgeois that has sprouted from the ruins of feudal society has not done away with class antagonism. It has but established new classes, new conditions of oppression and new forms of struggle in place of the old ones."¹

"Who are these classes of which you speak?" Thaddeus questioned.

"We have the bourgeois, the owner of all the capital. Then we have the modern working class, the proletariat, who live only so long as they find work. They must sell themselves piecemeal as a commodity, like every other article of commerce.

Owing to the extensive use of machinery and to the division of labour, the work of the proletarian has lost all individual character, all charm for the workman. He becomes an appendage of the machine and it is only the most simple, most monotonous and most easily acquired knack that is required of him.

Modern industry has converted the little workshops of the patriarchal master into the great factories of the industrial capitalist. Masses of labourers, crowded into the factories are organized like soldiers, placed under the command of a perfect hierarchy of officers and sergeants. Not only are they enslaved to the bourgeois class and bourgeois state, they are daily and hourly enslaved to a machine."²

"Sir, what do you propose?"

"The immediate aim of the Communists is the same as that of all the other proletarian parties. It is the formation of the proletariat into a class in order to overthrow the bourgeois supremacy and the conquest by the proletariat."³

"How do you propose that to happen?"

"We will abolish private property."⁴

"Sir, surely you do not expect people to simply hand over their property!" Thaddeus thought of Riverview Farm and Miller & Pierce Law Firm which had been in the family for generations.

"The solution is revolution!" Observing the young American's shock he challenged "Did not your country have a revolution?"

"Taxation without representation was the principle for which we fought," he corrected. "Look at the French Revolution. That did not end so well."

"The French Revolution abolished feudal property in favour of bourgeois property. Their revolution was incomplete. Property in its present form is based on the antagonism of capital and the wage earner.[5] The abolition of private capital will be converted into common property of all members of society."

Thaddeus shook his head. "Someone needs to own it. Someone needs to be responsible for the maintenance and upkeep of property."

"So you are horrified at our intending to do away with private property. In your existing society private property is already done away with for nine-tenths of the population; its existence for the few is solely due to its non-existence in the hands of the nine-tenths."

"Who exactly will own this non private property?"

"The state will own it all. The state will care for the poor."

"The church is to care for the poor," Thaddeus contradicted.

"Religion!" he scoffed. "Religion is the opiate of the masses. Religion is the means by which the oppressors perpetrate superstitions and myths to mollify the oppressed with empty promises of an afterlife."

"Members of the family care for one another. Grandparents help care for their young grandchildren, and in return the children and grandchildren help care for them decades later. That is the way it has always been done," Thaddeus argued.

"We intend to abolish the family! On what foundation is the present bourgeois family based? On capital and private gain. The bourgeois family will vanish as a matter of course with the vanishing of capital."[6]

Thaddeus was furiously scribbling down his notes. "Sir, other than translating *The Communist Manifesto* into English, how do you propose I educate my readers to your beliefs? Could you narrow down your manifesto into ten principles?"

"That is easily done." He sat back in his chair and silently stared into space for a moment before speaking.

"1. The abolition of private property
2. A heavy progressive, graduated income tax
3. The abolition of all right of inheritance
4. The confiscation of property of all emigrants and rebels
5. The centralization of credit in the hands of the State by means of a national bank with state capital as an exclusive monopoly
6. The centralization of the means of communication and transportation in the hands of the State
7. The extension of factories and instruments of production owned by the State and the bringing into cultivation of wasteland and in the improvement of the soil in accordance with a common plan
8. The equal liability of all labour. The establishment of industrial armies, especially for agriculture
9. The combination of agriculture with manufacturing industries; the gradual abolition of the distinction between town and country by a more equitable distribution of the population over the country
10. Free education for all children in public schools and the abolition of child factory labour"

"In summary, young man, we plan to form a stateless and classless society." [7]

"Sir, I still do not understand how you propose that all of this will be accomplished."

"The proletariat might be compelled to organize as a class, form a revolution, make itself a ruling class and sweep away old conditions of production."[8]

"Sir, you will make the oppressed into the new oppressors."

"We are merely redistributing the capital more fairly. Nothing more and nothing less. Good day, Mr. Pierce." He arose from his desk and nodded toward the door.

"Good day, Mr. Marx."

Thaddeus left the flat that afternoon uncertain if he had interviewed a genius or a madman.

VII

The General Store

Darian was excited to be accompanying Isaac, Rachel and their mother to Evans' General Store in the village. He helped Isaac load the wagon with sacks of goose feathers, baskets of eggs, and a small barrel of butter. He and Isaac walked along the loaded wagon during the short trip from the farm to the store. Darian helped Rachel down from the wagon just as he had seen the Miller men help the Miller ladies down from the wagon hundreds of times before.

Mr. Evans eagerly opened the front door. "It is a beautiful October afternoon. Mrs. Miller, may I be of any assistance?"

"Sir, if you would be so kind as to bring in the eggs, I believe the boys can handle everything else." Katherine Willey Miller may not have been as wealthy and renowned as Sadie, or as dignified and gracious as Grace or an outspoken abolitionist and leader of the Temperance Movement like Hannah, but she was respected as an industrious farmer's wife and a successful business woman. She need not buy anything with cash here for her credit was better than gold.

Darian remembered to remove his straw hat before entering the store. Some of the ladies who crowded the aisle smiled. "Hannah Miller will turn that wild Irish boy into a gentlemen and scholar yet," Mrs. Abbot whispered.

The General Store

"Let us hope she will lead him from his popish ways. He still refuses to attend church," Mrs. Osgood shook her head ruefully.

The boys carefully laid everything upon or near the front counter where Mr. Evans recorded each item in his day book, a leather-bound ledger. "You have a sizable credit in your account," he observed.

"That is indeed good news, for I have a sizable shopping list," she placed a neatly written paper down on the counter. Please do not add my butter to the barrel mixed with everyone else's and cart it off to Portland."

"Mrs. Miller I would be a fool to do so. All of Fryeburg is willing to pay a premium price for your butter," he smiled.

A bell jingled as the door opened. "I see we are having a family reunion," Mr. Evans greeted as Grace and Hannah entered the shop. "Are you ladies out for your daily walk on this beautiful day?"

"It is truly a glorious day. I have come to post this letter for my husband," Hannah handed him a letter addressed to John Quincy Adams.

How is the good Senator?"

"He is much fatigued, but of sound mind and of good spirits. Thank you for asking."

"Please tell Senator Miller, a number of us miss his lively political discussions around the pot belly stove. You know the national election is just weeks away. Perhaps he would care to stop by and enlighten us," Peter Evans, the youngest son of the family, warmly invited. "I will provide the coffee," he added.

"Peter, you are too kind," Hannah smiled. "I will extend the invitation and have my daughter drop him off some afternoon. I know he will enjoy the company.

I shall let you return to the business at hand." Hannah patted Kate on the arm. "I do not know what I would do without my daughter-in-law."

"You would be forced to eat your daughter's cooking," Grace quipped to the amusement to those within ear shot.

Mr. Evans took Kate's list and turned to the floor-to-ceiling shelves directly behind the counter. He pulled out one bin and measured five pounds of rice on the large brass scale and scooped it into a muslin bag. He scooped ten pounds of oatmeal into a small burlap sack. He knew the Millers never bought white sugar from the Caribbean plantations because it would have been picked by slaves. Then again, Micah Miller would produce enough maple sugar for the entire Miller family and still sell the extra to the store.

He then turned to his spice cabinet where he opened a small drawer of pepper corns, weighed them out and placed them into a small draw string bag. And he continued with handfuls of cloves, a bag of cinnamon sticks and a bag of nutmeg cloves. "Are you planning to mull some cider?"

"It promises to be a banner year," Kate replied. "My son, Daniel, will be in to pick up some nails. Please put them on this account."

"I will put a fifty pound sack of wheat flour in your wagon.[1]

Mrs. Miller, I have a business proposition for you. I wish to establish a small apothecary on the premises. Many women no longer grow the variety of medicinal herbs that their grandmothers once did. Could I interest you in becoming my local supplier? I believe we may come to a mutually agreeable financial arrangement," Peter asked. An intelligent and ambitious young man he was always striving to expand and to improve the family business. What Peter did not mention was the supplier in Portland wanted more than he was willing to pay and he hoped to get a better price from Kate.

"Sir, please continue."

As Kate conversed with Peter, Rachel wistfully fingered the bolts of colorful, printed cotton fabric.

The General Store

Mrs. Evans approached, "Rachel this pink and blue floral design would look lovely with your dark hair. Let me lay it out for you to take a closer look."

"Rachel, what are you doing?" Kate scolded.

"I thought perhaps I might make a new dress," she explained.

"With the new textile mills just down the river in Biddeford, the prices of these fine fabrics are very economical, indeed. I was just commenting how lovely this fabric would look with Rachel's dark hair," Mrs. Evans smiled.

"I am quite done shopping for the day, thank you. Come along, Rachel."

Rachel silently brooded on the ride home and waited until she was home before she confronted her mother. "I am not a child! I work just as hard as you on this farm and I deserve a new dress!"

"Dear, you do not need a new dress. You have an armoire filled with beautiful dresses that you never wear," Kate patiently explained.

"Those dresses are twenty-year old hand me downs from Sadie. They are silk and empire waist and old fashion. I want a cotton dress with mutton sleeves and with a matching bonnet."

"Rachel, there is a big difference between what we need and what we want. None of my children ever went without something they needed."

"I think I should be paid for my work here on the farm. Then I will decide for myself what I need."

"You know that is not how life works. We first provide for ourselves. Then we barter extra cider, produce and maple sugar with Daniel who supplies us with firewood. We exchange our wares and produce at the general store for needed items. You are worth far more than rubies, but your father and I cannot pay you cash for your labors. You should be more grateful for what you have. Look at those poor starving families in Ireland!"

"I do not live in Ireland. And I am grateful for what I have."

"Rachel, there will always be people who have more than we do and those who have less. We must learn to be content with what we have," Kate quietly admonished.

"I am going out!" Rachel turned to leave.

Kate sighed. "It is a beautiful afternoon. Enjoy your walk."

Rachel let herself in the back door of her grandparents' home. "Hello, Grandpa," she called.

"I am in the front parlor," Benjamin replied. "I am afraid that Nana and Aunt Grace have not returned from their walk. Grace is convinced that the workers cannot complete that church without her daily supervision," he laughed.

"I came to see you," she earnestly replied.

"I am indeed flattered," he motioned to her to sit down. "Please tell your old grandpa what has upset you."

"Promise me you will not think I am being silly."

"Never!" he replied.

"I would like to buy some fabric to make a new dress. Mother refuses because I have an armoire filled with Sadie's twenty-year old hand me downs and she does not feel I need a new dress. Also I think I should be paid for my work on the farm and then I could buy my own fabric. She refuses to do that. She is an impossible woman."

"Do not be hard on your mother. After all she has raised three sons who would have worn the same outfit every day for a year if she had let them. I have raised a son and a daughter and trust me there is a big difference. Perhaps she has forgotten that daughters may have different needs than sons.

Please harness the horse to the carriage and we shall go shopping."

"Mama will say you spoil me," she warned.

"It is my solemn obligation to spoil my only granddaughter. Who bought you your first porcelain doll? Who

The General Store

bought you the piano forte? A few yards of fabric should not matter!" he laughed jovially.

"Senator," Peter Evans greeted. "Have you come to discuss the upcoming election?"

"This is not a social visit, Peter. I have been sweet talked into buying some fabric. I assume this will entail thread and buttons and lace and other notions. If you are going to make one dress, you may as well make two. Yes, Mrs. Evans, that pink and blue fabric will look lovely with her dark hair. Yes, I will take the pale green fabric with the white flowers as well. Do you think we will need some ribbons with that?

Mrs. Evans, please help me select some fabric for my dear wife. Something pretty, but will not offend her Quaker sensibilities. Yes, this soft gray fabric with the light pink roses will suit her just fine.

Now Rachel, I will barter this fabric with your sewing a dress for your grandmother. I will not be accused of spoiling you," Benjamin grinned. He handed Mrs. Evans a half eagle. "Will this cover it?"

"Sir, let me get you your change."

"Just credit my account. Peter, please tell the gentleman I shall be here Monday afternoon promptly at one o'clock to discuss the election."

Rachel picked up the bundle with one hand and took her grandfather's arm with the other. Peter went ahead to open the door and to assist Benjamin into the carriage.

"Thank you, young man. I should get out more often. I will see you on Monday."

Kate was relieved when Rachel returned home in good spirits and helped prepare supper. "I spent the afternoon with Grandpa. He seemed lonely. I told him that I would drive him to Evans General Store on Monday to discuss politics. I think I should spend more time with him. Everyone seems to be too busy for him these days."

"That is very thoughtful of you. I am sure that if we manage our time well, I could spare you a few hours a day to spend with your grandparents."

Rachel smiled.

Rachel escorted Aunt Grace down to her grandparents shortly after 12:30 on Monday afternoon. "Hello, Grandpa. I will hitch the horse to the carriage. Grandpa, look at you all dressed up."

He grinned. "I grabbed this suit from the back of my armoire. I was saving it for my funeral. I thought it would not hurt if I wore it a few times before."

"You are dressed like John Quincy Adams," Grace teased.

"You are mistaken, dear Grace. John Quincy Adams is dressed like me."

"It is too windy to take a walk," Grace pronounced. "I suggest that we devote the afternoon to some sewing." Grace laid out the pink floral fabric across the long dining room table.

When Rachel and Benjamin arrived at the general store they found a dozen men gathered around the wood stove. "Good day, gentlemen," Benjamin greeted as he placed his hat on the nearby counter top. "This year's election proves to be an interesting one."

"You say that every four years," a voice in the back joked.

"Jedidiah, since when did you get interested in politics?" Benjamin replied good-naturedly.

"Since old man Evans started making coffee!"

"Grandpa, I will pick you up later," Rachel whispered as she quietly left the store.

"When I was elected to the United States Senate back in '24 John Quincy Adams served as the sixth President of the United States. Then he was defeated in the election of '28 by Andrew Jackson, a Democrat." Benjamin had a way of making the name of Andrew Jackson sound like a curse word. "After two terms of Jackson, Democrat Martin Van Buren from New York State was elected in '36.

The General Store

Old Tippecanoe, William Henry Harrison, was the first Whig elected to the Presidency eight years ago. He died of pneumonia exactly one month after taking office and Vice President John Tyler succeeded to the office. President Tyler lost his bid for the Presidency to Democrat, James Knox Polk four years ago. The recent annexation of Texas was completed during his Presidency.[2]

This is where our story gets interesting. President Polk has kept his promise of being a one term President. Therefore, there is no incumbent. This is not a simple race between two parties – the Democrats and the Whigs."

"It looks pretty simple to me," Asa Abbot argued.

"Asa, everything looks pretty simple to you," Mr. Evans joked. "Have another cup of coffee."

"There is a split in the Democratic Party. Remember that President Polk, a native from North Carolina is a Jacksonian Democrat. Polk's wing of the party is pro slavery. Martin Van Buren's wing of the party is anti-slavery. Their opponents call them 'Barnburners' accusing them that they would be willing to burn down the Democrats' barn in order to rid it of its proslavery rats."[3]

They nominated Michigan Senator Lewis Cass."

"He is a northerner, so that is good, right?" one man questioned.

"He is a northerner, but he promotes 'popular sovereignty' which states people of each territory have the right to decide for themselves whether slavery would be legal in their territory. This opens the possibility to the expansion of slavery in the territories of California or Oregon."[4]

"What about the Whigs?"

"The Whigs also have a strong anti-slavery wing led by the Conscience Whigs in Ohio and Massachusetts. I consider myself to be a Conscience Whig. This summer they nominated national hero, General Zachary Taylor. He has a glorious war record in the Mexican War and an unknown political record. What I do know is that General Taylor was born in Virginia, raised in Kentucky in an aristocratic, slave-holding family and presently owns a plantation with over one hundred slaves.[5] He also helped conquer a vast new expanse of territory for the spread of slavery."

"It sounds like we have a choice between a northern Democrat and a slave-holding Whig. What is the lesser of two evils?" Mr. Weston asked.

"We have a third party called the Free Soil Party," Benjamin explained.

"Is that legal?" someone asked.

"The Constitution does not prohibit it."

"Who did the Free Soil Party nominate?"

"They nominated Martin Van Buren for President and Charles Francis Adams for Vice President."

"I thought Martin Van Buren was already President."

"He was."

"Is that legal?"

"Several other Presidents ran for a second term in office," Benjamin noted.

"Yes, but the others never changed political parties. Is that legal?"

"Changing political parties is not prohibited by the Constitution."

"That means this is a three way race and not a two way race. What happens if none of the candidates win the majority of the Electoral College votes?" Peter Evans asked.

"Gentlemen, that is why this election is so interesting!"

"Did he say you have to go to college to get elected?"

"No, Asa. He said the Electoral College!" Mr. Weston corrected.

The bell jingled as Rachel entered to bring her grandfather home. Benjamin smiled with relief. "Saved by the bell," he laughed.

VIII
The Journey to Biddeford

Kate, Jacob, Eli, Rachel, Grace and Sadie quickly ate the noon meal on Tuesday. "Kate, is Rachel available to spend the afternoon with me at Hannah's? We are doing some sewing and she has the best eyesight to thread our needles," Grace asked.

"I can think of no better way for Rachel to spend an afternoon than with her grandparents," Jacob nodded. "I remembered when Abigail would spend hours visiting with our grandmother. That was a special time for both of them."

Unfortunately Kate could think of better ways for Rachel to spend the afternoon. There were root vegetables and apples to pick, herbs to dry. As reading his wife's mind, Jacob added, "If Darian has completed his studies please send him up for Eli and I can find much work to do. Kate dear, Isaac will be home from school soon. Everything will get done," he assured.

"Thank you, Papa. Grandpa's newspaper from Portland arrives by mail on Tuesdays. He will be most anxious for me to run to the general store to pick it up."

"And then he will be most anxious to read it aloud to us while we are trying to talk and sew!" Grace shook her head.

Grace and Rachel found Darian sitting at the kitchen table practicing his penmanship in his copy book. Book 4 of the

McGuffey's Readers lay opened on the kitchen table. Abigail was hurriedly washing the noon dishes.

"Darian, you have a fine hand," Grace complimented.

"Mr. Miller says it is important for a man to have good penmanship. 'The pen is mightier than the sword' he says. I have no idea what that means."

"Most of the time I have no idea what he means, either," Grace agreed.

"Mrs. Miller thinks I should be all caught up and ready to go to the stone school house next year. She says I am the best student she ever had," he boasted.

"Pride goeth before the fall," Hannah warned as she entered the kitchen.

"Yes, mam," he replied glumly.

"Nana, if Darian has completed his studies, my father could surely use his help."

Hannah laughed at his eager grin. "Please run to the general store to pick up Mr. Miller's newspaper and the mail before you leave for the farm."

"One moment please. After Mr. Miller signs these papers, I need you to take them to be mailed," Abigail wiped her hands on a linen towel and left for the office.

"I do not know what we would do without her," Hannah sighed. "Now with Joshua spending so much time in court, she practically runs the office by herself. She spent most of the morning writing up some wills and deeds."

"Is that legal?" Rachel asked in surprise.

"It is as long as Grandpa or Uncle Joshua reads it over, approves and signs it," Hannah explained.

Abigail handed the sealed documents to Darian. "What did we do without you?"

Beaming with pride, Darian took the documents and ran out the back door.

The Journey to Biddeford

"I hope you will not mind that Abigail and I took the liberty to do some sewing last evening," Hannah smiled." I think we may finish your dress by bedtime."

"After years of sewing shirts and trousers for Thaddeus, it is a delight to sew dresses for a young lady," Abigail added. "Your mother is so busy on the farm and in the kitchen. We should have thought years ago to start a sewing circle."

"Abigail, you are just as busy as Kate. No one recognizes it," Grace stated.

"Well, I for one certainly recognize and appreciate it," Benjamin interrupted. "Joshua always said that having Abigail in the office is like having a third partner."

Darian ran in the back door with his arms full. "Sir, you have your Portland newspaper and these books."

"My books came in!" Abigail quickly grabbed the package. "This winter I intend to initiate a reading club and I have selected *The Last of the Mohicans*."

"That is a brilliant idea! Winters are dreadfully dull," Grace complained.

"Darian, we will read this together. I believe you will enjoy it," Benjamin offered. "Rachel, did you know that your Aunt Abigail was an instructress at Fryeburg Academy before she married? I believe you would make a wonderful instructress as well. I shall discuss this with your father."

Rachel could not think of anything more exciting than to be out of the house all day and to earn and to spend her own money!

"Now run up to the farm," Hannah encouraged Darian.

"Oh, I almost forgot. Mrs. Pierce, you have a letter from Thaddeus from Paris."

"Paris, Maine?"

"No. Paris, France."

Abigail eagerly ripped open the letter and silently read the contents. "He intends to spend the winter in Paris writing," she reported glumly.

"You mean he intends to spend the winter sewing his wild oats on the Left Bank," Grace replied tartly.

"Grace!" Hannah gasped. "Darian, you may leave for the farm now."

"The French are simply the most immoral, lazy, self-important people. I remember Abigail Adams being simply shocked by Parisian society when she went to live with her husband in 1784."[1]

"It is not proper to judge an entire country based on the behavior of a few. That was decades ago, before the French Revolution," Hannah countered.

"Mark my words, Abigail; your husband should demand that he return immediately."

"Perhaps we should begin our sewing," Rachel suggested.

Rachel was most animated at the evening meal. "Did you know that Aunt Abigail was an instructress at Fryeburg Academy for years before she married? Do you know she practically runs the legal practice while Uncle Joshua is away at court and Grandpa is retired? She writes wills and deeds and everything! That must be why she always has ink stains on her index finger. Do you know she is starting a reading circle this winter? Anyone who wants to may join. We are going to read *The Last of the Mohicans*. Aunt Abigail is one of the most fascinating women I have ever met!

I never knew how interesting Nana is. Do you know she started her own school in Washington City teaching free blacks? I dare say she also taught some not-so-free ones as well. Do you know that Darian is already reading at Level 4? She is a wonderful teacher!"

"I must tell you it is amazing what women in America can accomplish when they are not in the kitchen all day," Grace quipped as she helped herself to a second helping of chicken and dumplings and butternut squash.

Kate held her tongue. "I am pleased that you appreciate your family," Jacob smiled. "If you are willing to help your mother this evening, I am sure we may spare you a few hours tomorrow afternoon for another visit."

"Grandpa, Nana and Aunt Abigail all think I would make a wonderful instructress at the academy. Nana says teaching is the most rewarding vocation one may have. I intend to teach next summer."

"Teaching certainly runs in the family," Jacob carefully chose his words.

"Rachel, summer is my busiest time on the farm. I cannot spare you!" Kate argued.

"There is no reason why Julia cannot be here every day in the summer to help. She lives just over the bridge. Rebecca and Victoria are certainly old enough to learn to help," Grace interjected. "Clearly Rachel has other interests."

"Thank you, Aunt Grace. We shall discuss this matter privately," Jacob ended the conversation. "We have picked baskets full of herbs and apples today. Perhaps the entire family could spend this evening together, peeling, coring and slicing apples to hang to dry. I for one would enjoy sitting down for a few hours. Sadie, perhaps you could hang them from the beams in an attractive manner. I think that would make a nice painting."

"Jacob, that is a brilliant idea! A New England Hearth at Harvest shall be the title," Sadie responded enthusiastically. "Mother, if you would wash the dishes this evening that would give the rest of us more time to work."

Grace replied, "I must tell you I would happily wash the dishes every evening in exchange for Rachel spending the afternoons with us."

There was no further discussion about Fryeburg Academy that evening. Jacob and Isaac sat together tying bunches of lemon balm, bee balm, anise hyssop, yarrow, sage and thyme as Sadie carefully hung them from the beams. Kate and Rachel wordlessly prepared the apples in awkward silence while Grace washed, dried put away the dishes and swept the floors. The family wearily went to bed well after the great clock in the drawing room struck eleven.

Abigail eagerly greeted her niece at the back door the next afternoon, "We have a surprise for you!" She held up the newly completed dress. "Go try it on!"

The family gathered around Rachel admiringly.

"Mrs. Evans is indeed correct. The dress does look lovely with your dark hair," Benjamin complimented.

"You look stylish and becoming, yet modest," Hannah approved.

"I shall surprise my family and wear it to church on Sunday," Rachel said.

"Shall we begin the green dress?" Grace suggested.

"No, we should begin Nana's dress today. Then both of us shall wear our new dresses on Sunday," Rachel concluded. "The green dress may wait."

"Darian, please inform my son that you have our permission to spend the night at the farm in order to help with the evening chores. Be sure to return right after breakfast for your studies," Hannah instructed. "Mind your table manners."

He grinned impishly, "I know. I was not raised in a barn." If the truth be told the hovel in which he was raised was no match for the local barns. Although he greatly respected the kind, elderly couple who provided him with a home and education, life at the farm was much more exciting. He grabbed his straw hat and ran out the back door. He immediately returned, "Thank you, mam. Is there anything you need done before I leave?"

Benjamin nodded his approval, "If you would be kind enough to bring in one more bucket of water from the well and two arms' worth of firewood for the wood box."

"Yes, sir. A man needs to take care of the family," If only Darian could have taken care of his own family.

As the ladies rolled out the fabric on the dining room table Rachel glumly announced, "Mother needs me in the summer and will not consent to me teaching at the academy."

"Your mother is the hardest working woman I have ever met and I do not question her need of assistance during the summer," Hannah began diplomatically. "Perhaps she has grown too dependent upon you when there are other members of this family who could help."

"I must tell you I washed and dried the dishes last night," Grace interjected.

"That is wonderful. Perhaps you and Sadie could wash the dishes every evening. I am no spring chicken but I am certainly cable of helping out during harvest. My own dear mother-in-law helped on the farm in any way she could. Please tell your mother I will be there Saturday morning to assist her. Next year once Darian is in school I shall have more time to devote at the farm. Perhaps in the meantime Grace you could find ways to help in the mornings."

"I could set the table at mealtimes," Grace offered.

Rachel was only half listening as she thumbed through her grandfather's newspaper. The following advertisement caught her attention:

Laconia Mills in Biddeford seeking dependable, hardworking young ladies to work spinning machines and looms in modern textile mill. Safe, clean boarding houses located nearby providing three meals per day and proper chaperoning.

She jotted down the information on a scrap of paper and hid it in her apron pocket.

That evening Grace set the dining room table with her mother's china as Kate and Rachel brought in the meal. "Why are we eating in the dining room? It is not Sunday," Isaac asked. "Your mother has spent the entire day in the kitchen

The Fryeburg Chronicles Book IV

and I thought it would be nice to eat in the dining room," Grace explained. "Kate, Hannah will be here on Saturday to help you with things."

"Why thank you, Aunt Grace." Kate was unsure how to respond to Grace's new-found generosity.

Darian made sure he placed his linen napkin in his lap before Jacob gave thanks. "Lord we thank you for this good harvest and this good family and for your unending love for us. Amen."

"What is on the evening's chore list?" Grace asked.

"Well, we picked the rest of the apples and all the pumpkins and squash and filled half of the root cellar," Jacob began. "It feels like a frost tonight. Tomorrow we will pick some turnips, potatoes and beets and get those in. Tonight we will finish the barn chores and turn in early. I do not think I can stay up past eleven two nights in a row."

"I think if we can clean and organize the kitchen tonight, Rachel and I will be up early to do the baking," planned Kate.

"On Saturday we will make cider on the old cider press. The hayloft is filled and by tomorrow night the root cellar will be filled. By Saturday night we will have enough cider to last the year," Jacob declared with satisfaction.

"Then will we be ready for the winter?" Darian innocently asked. Ever since his arrival in May, all he ever heard from the Millers was 'getting ready for winter'. He had no idea what that meant.

"We will be half way ready. On Monday Danny will begin to deliver twenty cords of firewood in exchange for a winter's worth of root vegetables and cider. Then we need to stack the wood in the woodshed. Eli will help us and then we will go across the river and help him with his."

Isaac groaned. He knew for the next month he will be either in school, in bed or stacking firewood. "Perhaps with Darian's help it will only take half as long," he thought wistfully.

"When the wood is in, it is time to go hunting. That is always best with a few inches of snow on the ground. I thought you two boys are about the age to learn to hunt."

Darian had no idea what animals they would be hunting. Do they shoot beavers? He hoped not. He had grown fond of the family of beavers he and Isaac visited on a weekly basis. Do they shoot those huge animals with the big antlers? He had only seen two of these awkward and homely animals in the woods. Admittedly a moose could feed the entire Miller clan. He had heard coyotes at night but had never seen one.

Isaac was thrilled. "It is about time! Eli and Danny were younger than me when Papa and Uncle Micah took them hunting."

"When Mama and I are done with the dishes, I will bake some apples," Sadie offered. "Winter is long enough for me to paint, but harvest passes quickly."

The entire Miller clan gathered at the farm after breakfast on Saturday. Julia and daughters Rebecca and Victoria, Rachel and Emily dumped baskets of apples into the apple crusher as Isaac, Darian and Davy took turns turning the handle and then dumping the apple mash into the cider press. Jacob, Eli and Daniel took turns turning the large screw which slowly lowered the press onto the apple mash. After Joshua collected the buckets filled with cider he began filling the newly washed stoneware jugs. The older ladies stayed in the kitchen cooking and baking and feeding the thirteen hungry Millers.

Only Benjamin sat alone in his father's old wing back chair in the parlor and watched his family through the eight-paned window. He closed his eyes and dozed.

At sunset, the head of each family loaded his wagon with jugs of cider. Isaac and Darian also helped Daniel load his wagon with root vegetables. Joshua paid cash for their vegetables, cider and firewood. Wearily they called good night to one another with promises of seeing each other in church the next morning.

Sunday morning Rachel came to breakfast wearing her new pink and blue print dress with the mutton sleeves. Kate gasped, "I told you we could not afford that fabric. Did you put that on my account?" she accused.

"Katherine, she did no such thing," Grace assured. "She bartered with her grandfather some fabric for sewing a dress for her grandmother."

"That is what you have been doing behind my back all week? Sewing a dress I told you that you could not have?"

"You said you could not afford it. You did not say I could not have it," Rachel replied steely. "You barter for your goods and I barter for mine. That is the Miller's way. I am a grown woman and no one will tell me what I may and may not own."

"When you live under our roof..."

Jacob and Isaac could hear the yelling from the barn and came running in.

"Katherine, you are being unreasonable," Grace warned.

"Kate, what is wrong?" Jacob asked. She pointed to Rachel. "That dress looks pretty with your dark hair. It is a very modest dress and appropriate for Sunday worship. Harvest time should be a time of gratitude. I fear we have allowed the extra work and exhaustion get the better of us. Let us put away our frustrations and go to church. I think some hymns, prayers and a good sermon is what this family needs right now. I fear I have become somewhat lax with our family Scripture reading and this is the result.

My sister Abigail has invited us and Danny and Emily over for Sunday dinner. There will be no talk about her cooking. She knows this is a busy time for all of us, and she wishes to relief Kate of the duties of cooking Sunday dinner."

The family quietly sat in their pew with Kate and Rachel each seething in indignation. Isaac sat by his father doing his best not to fidget. Benjamin had volunteered to stay home and keep the Sabbath with Darian. Hannah, wearing her new dress, sat with Abigail and Joshua.

Upon arrival from church the family found Benjamin and Darian seated by the parlor stove in the law office where Darian was tentatively reading aloud from St. Patrick's Confession.

The house burst into activity. Joshua and Daniel stabled the horses, Grace and Sadie set the table in the dining room, Isaac and Darian brought in water and firewood for the cook stove, Emily and Rachel assisted Abigail in bringing the meal. "Kate, you sit and relax," Hannah instructed. Benjamin prayed a long and elegant blessing while Darian's stomach growled. He much preferred Jacob's short and simple prayers at meal times.

No one complained that the cream of potato soup lacked seasoning, the biscuits were slightly burned on the bottom, or the baked apples were rather dry for they had plenty of sweet cider to drink.

"I shall miss Sunday dinners when I move to Biddeford at the end of the month," Rachel broke the silence. She had hoped that her parents would not dare argue with her in front of the family. Daniel and Emily silently looked at one another.

"Rachel, you know I need you to help with the creamery and keeping house. That is simply out of the question," Kate answered struggling to keep her voice calm.

"Nana says that you are far too dependent upon me when there are other family members who could help," Rachel countered.

Hannah blushed.

"Why do you wish to leave for Biddeford?" Jacob asked softly.

"I shall be a spinner at Laconia Mill and live in a nearby boarding house. Thousands of young women are leaving the farms to work in the mills and earn their own money."

"Rachel, we Millers work for ourselves. We do not allow others to profit by our labors," Benjamin sternly responded.

"Those mills are spinning and weaving cotton picked by slaves. You should not profit from slave labor," Hannah admonished.

"You are wearing a new cotton dress," Rachel pointed out to her grandmother. "People will buy and wear cotton regardless if I work in a mill or not. Slavery will not end if I choose to remain home!"

"Your place is here with the family until you have a family of your own," Jacob reminded.

"Please, do not leave," Isaac whined.

Rachel stood up to leave. "Thank you Aunt Abigail for dinner, but I must head back."

Kate looked to Jacob to intervene but he remained silent. After fifteen minutes he announced, "Now that she has had some time to herself, I will go talk to her. Isaac, please hitch up the horses when Aunt Grace, Sadie and your mother are ready to go home. Please excuse me."

Jacob found his daughter sitting on her bed staring out the window. "I do not wish to speak of this," she warned.

Jacob sat by Rachel's side. "I regret you never met my grandfather James Miller. They do not make men like him anymore. He was a farmer like Uncle Micah, a carpenter and joiner like my Uncle Ethan and a Harvard graduate and scholar like my father. He had the Wisdom of Solomon and the Patience of Job. Your grandfather was always getting into trouble for reading books instead of doing his chores."

Rachel laughed. "I cannot picture Grandpa a young boy like Isaac."

"James had the wisdom to see that this son was not destined to become a farmer and he encouraged him to study after the chores. The good Lord has a sense of humor. My father, who grew to be a scholar, a headmaster and an attorney, had a son who hated school and reading! My grandfather had the wisdom to tell my father that he should encourage me to be a farmer."

"Did he?"

"Gradually he accepted who I was. I do not claim to be as wise as my grandfather, but I am wise enough to see that you are unhappy here. Perhaps you could live with your grandparents and become an instructress at the Academy. Your grandmother would appreciate your company and Aunt Abigail would appreciate a little help."

"No Papa, I am leaving at the end of the month."

"A father's job is to provide for and protect his daughter. If you leave for the mill, then I can do neither," he said sadly.

She put her hand on his arm, "You were a wonderful provider and protector when I was a girl. But I am an adult now and I can protect myself. Are you afraid I will meet some man sowing his wild oats?"

"Where did you hear such language?" Jacob asked shocked.

"Aunt Grace says Thaddeus is sowing his wild oats in Paris. Did you sow any wild oats?"

Jacob blushed. "I saved my oats for your mother. You are not always fair to her. She is the most talented, hardworking women I have ever known. She reminds me of my grandmother, Sarah Miller.

I have three sons – a farmer, a sawyer and one to help me in my old age; I depend upon them for different reasons. A woman like your mother could keep six daughters busy. I fear that you resent her dependence upon you. It is not easy for women to share a kitchen or for men to share a barn."

"You and Eli share a barn," she noted.

"Someday your brother will build his own barn. He has very strong opinions on how to run a farm. Having his own barn will give him the opportunity to practice those opinions.

You and your mother are not the only two with struggles. Families must develop patience with each other."

"I love you Papa. But I am still leaving for Biddeford."

The night before Rachel was due to leave, the Miller clan descended upon the farm.

"How will you get there? You know Mother, Father and Eli cannot leave for a two day trip at this time of year," Danny inquired.

"I am perfectly capable of taking the stage coach."

"Emily and I discussed this last night. We would like to take you in our wagon. This way she and I can help you get settled and drive home on Sunday," Danny offered.

"Here is a copy of *Last of the Mohicans*," Abigail handed her a book. "You could have your own reading circle in Biddeford."

"Please take my cloak. It has a hood and it is much warmer," Kate offered. "You will have to walk to the mill in all kinds of weather whereas I can work in the comfort of my kitchen."

Rachel had not considered that before. Reluctantly she accepted the gift. "Mama, please take my cloak in exchange." Emily had knitted her several pairs of wool stockings and Julia had sewn two wool petticoats. Eli handed her a pair or fur mittens.

"Thank you, Eli, but I have a pair of white wool mittens," Rachel reminded.

"When the thermometer reads below zero, you will need to wear the fur mittens over your wool mittens. Last January 11 it was 36° below zero!"[2] Since Eli purchased a thermometer last year at the general store he appointed himself to record the temperatures every day.

"Here is something to help you to remember home," Sadie gave her a small oil painting of Rachel as a young girl playing by the river.

Rachel fought back tears. "Thank you, I will treasure this always."

"Be sure to write to us every week," Hannah gave her a wooden box filled with paper, two quills and a bottle of ink.

Rebecca and Victoria shyly gave their aunt some hair ribbons. Finally Grace presented her with the green dress with the white flowers. "Your grandmother and I finished this yesterday. Abigail threaded the needles for us. You must keep at least one good dress for church," she reminded.

"Well thank you all. I shall be warm this winter. During the evenings I shall read and write letters home." Rachel stood up.

"Please play the piano one more time for your grandfather," Benjamin requested.

To Isaac's embarrassment he burst into tears.

"It's not like she died! She is only moving down river," Darian berated him.

Joshua silently observed the angry Irish boy.

"There will be room in the wagon tomorrow. Father, could Isaac accompany us? I would appreciate the help in moving the trunk." Danny asked.

"That is an excellent suggestion," Jacob agreed. "After our recital I believe this family needs to retire for the night. Tomorrow will be big day."

IX

The Boarding House

Before dawn the four sojourners began their travel south east following the course of the Saco River. Although Daniel had only seen the Fryeburg portion of the river, he knew it originated at Saco Lake in Crawford Notch in the White Mountains of New Hampshire before it crossed the Maine border in Fryeburg. After Fryeburg it continued in a south easterly direction through Hiram, Baldwin, Limington and Hollis and emptied in the Saco Bay and the Atlantic Ocean. Biddeford was located at the south side of the river and the town of Saco on the north side.

Uncle Joshua had drawn him a map with directions to Hooper's Inn on the Post Road in Biddeford. Benjamin slipped Daniel a $10.00 eagle and letter of introduction instructing him that the four of them should enjoy a hearty meal and a good night's rest before escorting Rachel to the boarding house. He also encouraged him not to travel on the Sabbath and to spend Sunday night at the inn as well.

Isaac was quite excited at the prospect of spending two nights at an inn. Emily quietly watched the landscape slowly pass, occasionally commenting on a farm house. Rachel filled with anticipation of freedom as they approached Hooper's Inn.

"I see we have another mill girl in town," the clerk greeted the family. Daniel handed the middle aged man the letter of introduction. "Sir, please let me help you with the trunk," he offered eagerly. "Will you be dining with us this evening as well?"

"Yes sir," Daniel replied.

Rachel resented that her grandfather had given the letter and money to Daniel instead of to her and that the clerk called her another 'mill girl', ignored her and directed his questions to Daniel. "Where is the closest house of worship?" she interrupted.

"That would be the Second Congregational Church.[1] Will you be having Sunday dinner with us as well?" The clerk struggled to help Daniel carry the trunk to the second floor where he showed them two small rooms with one bed in each overlooking a back alley. Being the only daughter of the family she had the privilege of having her own small bedroom back home and did not relish the thought of sharing her bed with her younger brother tonight. Well, it was only for one night. Beginning tomorrow she would once again have her own room.

The evening meal was no match to Mama's meals back home. "I think Aunt Abigail cooked this," Isaac giggled. It was the first time they had laughed all day. It was early to bed but Abigail could not sleep. Was it nerves or her brother's wiggling?

The next morning Rachel dressed in her new pink and blue cotton dress over two layers of wool petticoats and wool stocking. She donned her mother's cloak with the hood and headed off to the Second Congregational Church with her family. Rachel did not realize how much she would miss Reverend Hurd. Sunday dinner was a mediocre meal. Perhaps the food at the boarding house would be better.

"Could you direct us to the Laconia Mill?" Rachel asked the clerk before Daniel had the opportunity.

"Why do they call it Laconia?" Isaac asked." Laconia is in New Hampshire and we are in Biddeford."

"Because Samuel Batchelder named his mill after his hometown," the clerk explained.

"Who is Samuel Batchelder?" Rachel asked.

The clerk shook his head in disbelief. "Samuel Batchelder developed the Hamilton Mills in Lowell, Massachusetts then came to Biddeford and started the Saco Water Company with a group of investors. They developed the water power for the mills, they built a large machine shop that builds all the machinery for the mills and then he built the first cotton manufacturing company in Biddeford. The first two Laconia Mills were built in 1844 and went into operation in '45. The third mill was built last year. That must be the one you will be working. They employ 1,500 workers and the water company 600 men. They are building the Pepperell Mill now."[2]

Rachel could not imagine working with 1500 people nor could she imagine a building large enough to hold 1500 people.

Daniel grew interested." My saw mill in Fryeburg runs on water power."

The clerk looked at him with distain. "Batchelder hired Irish immigrants to dig canals perpendicular from the river. Then he hired Greek and Italian stone masons to build the foundations and arches from local rock. The canals actually run under the sub basements of the mills turning the water wheel which in turn run the machines.

The Saco Brick Yard on the other side of the river makes all the bricks for the mills and boarding houses."[3]

Rachel had never seen a brick building before. She knew that Lovell, the town next to Fryeburg, had a brick yard and there were several brick homes there. Now she would be living in a brick house. She stood up straight and cleared her throat, "Danny, I think it is best that we be on our way. Good day, sir."

"See you folks this evening," he replied.

The Boarding House

Isaac gasped as the three story buildings came into view. "I did not think it was possible to build a building so big! Rachel, are you going to work here? Will you get lost?"

Rachel swallowed the panic in her throat. "Once I am settled at the boarding house, I will ask for directions to the new Laconia Mill."

"I am certain that the other young ladies at the boarding house also work there. Tomorrow morning you can walk with them," Emily suggested. Rachel smiled at her in gratitude.

"According to Uncle Joshua's directions, this should be your boarding house," he stopped the carriage. "All these brick buildings on these city streets looked alike," he muttered. "I shall knock on the front door before I drag that trunk out again."

"Although Biddeford is much bigger than Fryeburg, it is certainly not larger than Buffalo. After a few days we learned our way around there. By mid- week Rachel will find her way as well," Emily assured.

"Danny and Emily, thank you for taking me. I do not know how I would have managed on my own in a stagecoach." She watched her brother knock at the front door and a stern, husky woman with her hair pulled back into a bun answered and then nodded.

Daniel ran back to the wagon. "Isaac, please help me with the trunk." The brothers trudged to the door. "Mrs. Libby, this is my sister Rachel Miller."

She studied Rachel carefully before speaking. "You look older than the rest of the girls."

"I am twenty-eight years old, mam. I do hope that will not be a problem."

"Not at all, Miss Miller. I trust you shall be more sensible than some of these young girls," she approved. "Mr. Miller, I assure you that I take excellent care of my girls. I provide three wholesome meals per day, I see to it that they are each properly chaperoned and go to church every Sunday.[4] I run the finest boarding house in Biddeford. If it was not for that unfortunate accident last week, I would not have had a vacancy.

This is the dining room," she nodded to a large, spacious room with two pine trestle tables each large enough to seat twenty people. The sitting room is where the girls may entertain their guests.[5]

"You have a piano!" Rachel walked over to the small upright.

"Do you play?"

Rachel sat down and played part of a piece by Chopin that she had committed to memory.

"Let me show you to your room," Mrs. Libby offered. The Millers followed her carrying the trunk to the third floor. "This is one of our nicer rooms," she opened the door. To Rachel's disappointment there were three beds, one dresser and some pegs upon which to hang her clothes. Trunks and bandboxes lined one wall. An oil lamp sat on a writing desk by the window. It was crowded but very tidy.

"There are three to a room?" Rachel tried to conceal her disappointment.

"Oh no. There are six to a room, two to a bed. This house has seven bedrooms including mine on the first floor. I will ask you gentlemen to please wait for your sister downstairs while she and Mrs. Miller unpack."

Rachel placed her box of stationary, quills, ink and her novel on the desk as Emily hung her green and white dress on a peg. There was only one vacant drawer in the dresser where she placed her stockings, aprons and mobcaps. "Perhaps we can slide the trunk under the bed for storage. We need not store all your things in the drawer," Emily suggested.

Daniel and Isaac went outside where Daniel tended the horses and Isaac sat on the stoop dejectedly. "Why would she rather live here than with us?" he put his head down and cried.

The Boarding House

Daniel sat down beside his brother and patted him on the back. "It will not be forever. Maybe after a few months when she has earned some money she may decide to return home. We cannot let Rachel see you cry."

Isaac dried his tears and put on a brave face as Emily and Rachel came to the door.

"It will soon be time for the evening meal," Rachel began. "I thank you for all your help. Isaac, be kind to Darian and listen to Mama. I promise I will write a letter at the end of the week."

Emily and Daniel warmly embraced her as Isaac stared down at the ground saying nothing. Rachel quickly turned and ran back into the boarding house before her family saw her tears.

"Are you settled in?" Mrs. Libby asked politely. She knew the first few days were difficult for new arrivals.

"May I set the table for you, mam?" Rachel offered as several of the young ladies began to appear for the evening meal. "My grandmother always says 'idle hands are the devil's workshop'." She smiled as she handed some plates to another diner.

"You must be new. Are you the girl taking Mary's place?" another boarder asked.

Mrs. Libby cleared her throat. "There will be plenty of time to chat. Rachel, we have assigned seating. You may take Mary's seat." She corrected herself, "This seat is reserved for you. I believe it is easier to become acquainted with your other housemates with assigned seating. You will spend plenty of time with your five roommates."

"Where did you learn to play the piano?" one girl who could not have been much older than fifteen asked wistfully.

"My grandfather bought me a piano when I was about your age and hired a teacher for me," she explained.

"Oh, are you rich?" someone asked.

"Rich girls do not last long. They are not accustomed to hard work," another sneered.

"My grandfather has been rather successful in life and takes pride in spoiling his only granddaughter," she smiled. "However I grew up on a farm working twelve to fourteen hour days. I help my mother run her creamery, the house and care for my little brother."

"Was that your brother who was crying on the step?"

"I fear so."

One plump girl in a brown dress asked, "Do you give piano lessons? I shall pay you of course."

Rachel looked to Mrs. Libby. "You may allocate one evening per week for lessons." The matron believed her boarding house should be a refining influence on her girls.

"Are you working to pay off the mortgage on the farm?" another girl in a thread bare dress asked.

"I am working to further my education at Mount Holyoke Female Seminary in Massachusetts. I wish to become a teacher. My grandparents were both educators and my Aunt Abigail was an instructress before she married my uncle. I guess teaching runs in the family. My aunt is initiating a reading circle back home."

Mrs. Libby looked at the newcomer thoughtfully. "I would enjoy a reading circle during the long winter months. Perhaps Rachel you would volunteer to read while the rest of us sews or embroiders."

"My aunt gave me a copy of *Last of the Mohicans*. We may begin with that and my grandfather could send me other books in the future."

A slender girl with light brown hair and a persistent cough shyly asked her, "Do you give reading lessons as well? When my mama got sick nine years ago, I had to leave school to care for the young ones at home. I would be right proud to learn to read and write real good. When my papa sent me here to work I was afraid I would never be able to go to school. Now I can still go to school and work."

"This week I will write my grandparents to ask for some teaching supplies. We can commence once I have the necessary items."

For the second night in a row Rachel Miller did not sleep well. She was startled by a bell that rang at 4:30 a.m.

"You will soon grow accustomed to the bells," her sixteen-year old bed mate explained.

Rachel had very little time to brush and put up her hair, without the aid of a looking glass.

"Do not fuss with your hair," one of her roommates chided. "Your mobcap will cover it all."

Rachel was a modest young woman, and not accustomed to dressing in front of others. In honor of her first day at work, she decided to wear her new green and white dress and her white apron over it. She was the last one at the dining room table.

"You will learn how to get ready quickly," Nancy, the young girl who had requested reading lessons, reassured as she ladled some oatmeal into her bowl. "Would you like some coffee?"

Being raised in a family of avid tea drinkers, she had never tasted coffee before. "I guess I could try some," she winced at the bitterness. The girls at the table laughed.

"Here, try some cream and sugar," someone offered.

She poured the cream right up to the rim. She hesitated at the sight of the white sugar. What would Nana say? Coffee beans and sugar cane were picked by slaves in the Caribbean. The Millers always used their own maple sugar and drank tea. Well, she was already wearing a dress made from cotton picked by slaves and she is working at a textile mill supplied with cotton picked by slaves, so did it matter? She stirred two heaping teaspoons in and enjoyed the first sip of the sweet, creamy beverage. To her astonishment another bell rang.

"That means it is time to leave," someone explained. She gulped her coffee, grabbed her cloak and mittens and followed her housemates out the door.

X

The Textile Mill

Rachel's housemates delivered her to the front office and hurried to their posts before the work bell rang. A supervisor efficiently wrote down some information and then simply said "Follow me."

Rachel obediently followed the woman through a maze of rooms and staircases until stopping in front of a large spinning machine. She was overwhelmed by her surroundings. The loud screeching of a hundred machines assaulted her ear drums. The floor boards actually trembled under her feet. The flying cotton lint, which at first looked like snow, clogged her airways causing her to cough. The heat and humidity felt like August.[1] She regretted dressing in her wool stockings and two wool petticoats.

As the floor lady approached, the supervisor silently left. It was futile to attempt a conversation in the midst of this industrial racket. Wordlessly the floor lady directed her to a long line of spinning bobbins. They walked the length of the bobbins as she pointed out two bobbins which were filled, pulled them off, dropped them in an awaiting basket, and replaced two empty wooden bobbins. She continued pacing the floor expertly observing each bobbin as they passed. Pointing to one bobbin where the thread had broken, she motioned to Rachel to tie a knot. Rachel tied the knot slowly and carefully and the bobbin began to spin. The floor lady frowned her disapproval and distinctly mouthed the words, "too slow" before continuing. She pointed to another bobbin which had filled and stopped and motioned to Rachel, who removed it, placed it in the basket and placed an empty bobbin.

The woman nodded and left her alone. "This is it? This is my job for the next thirteen hours staring at spinning bobbins?" she wondered. Rachel imagined what her family would be doing. Of course Daniel, Emily and Isaac would be leaving on their return trip home. Papa and Eli would be in the barn tending to the livestock.

Mama would be washing the breakfast dishes and then be drinking her second cup of tea. Perhaps she would fill her chests of herbs or do some sewing or sweeping or listen to Aunt Grace talk about her childhood in Boston. Sadie had begun a painting of her father and the family making maple syrup at their sugar house. Rachel wondered how that was coming along. Time passed slowly. Papa and Eli were probably taking a break and sitting at the Liberty Table enjoying some bread and butter to 'tide them over until the noon meal'.

She gasped when she noticed that five bobbins were filled and two had broken threads. When did that happen? She quickly replaced the filled bobbins and carefully retied the broken threads and continued to pace down the aisle. "I wonder what Grandpa is doing? Is he reading or is he napping in the front parlor? Of course Nana would be instructing Darian. Perhaps I could borrow the first levels of the McGuffey's Readers to teach Nancy. There are too many names to remember. Now I understand how Darian felt when he met all of us Millers last May." To her exasperation five more bobbins were filled.

A young man came to take the basket and looked at her with disgust and shook his head. Only then did she realize that the other girls' baskets were nearly filled. She would need to pay closer attention. The next hour she diligently watched the bobbins and a few times actually noticed it the moment it had

The Textile Mill

stopped. By the third hour her slender fingers could quickly tie the knots. By the fourth hour her head began to throb. She had not spoken a word to anyone since her arrival. She never realized how much she and her mother talked to one another in a day. Her stomach growled. She was not free to set aside her work for a few minutes to enjoy a biscuit. She had no idea what time it was; there was no clock in the front hall to ring out the hour and half hour. Her life was now measured by bobbins, not hours and minutes. Without warning, a bell loudly rang and girls began turning off their machines. She waved wildly to catch the floor lady's attention who walked over and showed her how to turn off the machine. She wearily descended the dusty staircase.

She panicked. Where did she hang her cloak? Was this the staircase she had taken earlier this morning? Will she be able to find her way back to the boarding house? To her relief she spied Nancy exiting the door and quickly followed her out. The cold air enveloped her as she shivered.

"Where is your cloak?"

"I do not know. In fact, I fear I will not be able to find my place after lunch," Rachel confessed.

Nancy laughed good- naturedly. "We all feel that way on the first day. I work four rows behind you. After lunch I will walk you to your station. You probably left your cloak in the office. At the end of the day we will check to see if it is still there."

A bell rang to signify it was time to eat as the girls all rushed into the boarding house's dining room. Rachel first raced to the privy. "Where is your cloak?" Mrs. Libby scolded. Throughout the meal Rachel worried that someone might steal it. How would she tell her mother? Of course she could not. She would take her money and buy herself a new one. Another bell rang announcing it was the end of meal time and in unison the girls all stood up and left. They had a total of forty-five minutes to leave the mill, walk to the boarding house, eat and return to the mill. Rachel felt it was rude to leave Mrs. Libby with all the dishes, but what could she do? She would offer to help with the dishes tonight.

Now she understood why the girls loudly chattered. It was to compensate for the hours of isolation. She dreaded returning to her station as the machines returned to life and filled the cavernous room with deafening noise. Her baskets of bobbins filled more quickly and the young man nearly smiled at the improvement. Her production continued to improve throughout the afternoon until she noticed the room began to slowly darken. The young man reappeared to light the oil lamps. The overpowering smell of whale oil began to nauseate her. Again, without warning, the bell rang. Simultaneously the machines ceased and Nancy hurried to Rachel's station.

"Be quick! We will run to the front office to grab your cloak and leave. It is not safe for the two of us to walk the streets alone after dark."

Rachel had not considered that. She often walked to her grandparents by the light of a lantern in the evenings. She thanked the supervisor for watching her cloak, quickly threw it on and rushed out the front door arm in arm with Nancy. They returned to the boarding house only a few minutes after the rest.

"I see you found your cloak," Mrs. Libby noticed.

"Yes, with Nancy's help."

"Will you play the piano for us?" someone asked.

"Not tonight. I have a headache."

"You will grow accustom to the mill," Mrs. Libby comforted.

"Not everyone does," another contradicted.

She ignored the chatter at the dinner table as she slowly ate the bland stew and day-old bread. She wondered if Daniel, Emily and Isaac had returned home yet. She wondered what her family was eating. She did not offer to help with the

The Textile Mill

dishes but wearily ascended the stairs to the third floor, quickly undressed and fell into bed.

The next morning she awoke before the bell, quickly poured some water from the pitcher into the wash basin, washed her face and hands, got dressed in cotton stockings and one cotton petticoat, brushed her curly brown hair and put in up into a bun. She decided to wear one of her old work dresses and to reserve her new dresses for special occasions. To her dismay, her feet were swollen as she struggled to get her shoes on. How would she ever survive for the next thirteen hours? She remembered her old deer skin moccasins Eli had made for her three years ago. During mud season her mother insisted that everyone wear their moccasins in the house and their shoes in the barn and outdoors. She quietly descended the two flights of stairs to the dining room.

"May I help you set the table?" she asked.

"You are up early."

"I am an early riser." The bell rang and the sounds of thirty-five young women scurrying to get ready could be heard. "I do hope you shall not be offended but I brought some chamomile tea. I am not accustomed to coffee and found its effects to be most disagreeable. My mother and I grow chamomile and make our own tea," she explained as she placed cups and bowls on the table. "How long have you run the boarding house?"

"This is my third year. I came two months after my husband was killed in an accident while building the second mill. My daughter lived with me until she married last year."

"My mother would approve – the house is efficiently run and immaculate. Your cooking is just like my Aunt Abigail's."

Mrs. Libby smiled her appreciation as thirty-five girls came bounding down the stairs. "Ladies! Walk, please. Perhaps I should serve everyone chamomile tea," she shook her head.

That morning Nancy walked her to the correct side door, led her up the two flights of stairs and to her station. "I will be right there," she pointed four rows behind. "When the lunch bell rings, walk back to my station." She hurried to her spot just as the work bell rang.

There was only one sound she despised more than the screeching machines and it was those detestable bells. The cotton stockings and petticoat only slightly decreased her discomfort in the heat. She was thankful she had eschewed her vanity in favor of her old moccasins as she began to pace the length of her spinning bobbins.

"I earn $3.00 per week for 73 hours of work in six days which means I make 50 cents per day or a little over 4 cents per hour. Room and board is $1.25 per week.[2] This amount is almost half of my earnings! I will never earn enough money to attend school!"

Three bobbins were filled and one thread needed to be tied. "I will have to give piano and reading lessons, no matter how tired I may be in the evening. I will charge 5 cents for a half hour lesson per pupil. That will go directly to my education fund." Six more bobbins were filled. "Should I deposit my money in the bank in town?" Fryeburg did not have a bank and it would be very cosmopolitan to have a bank account. "How would that be possible if I am at work during banking hours? How would I get the money in? How would I get the money out? Would Papa have to sign papers? I know how Grandpa feels about Andrew Jackson and the National Bank." She competently replaced ten bobbins and tied four knots.

"Where would I keep my money at the boarding house? Would it be safe? Would it get stolen? I will use my money to buy a lock and key for my trunk and keep the key around my neck. Grandpa told me sometimes banks fail. That would be safer? What happens if the house burns down then I would lose everything. But the house is brick so that should not happen."

The Textile Mill

She had not realized how hungry she was until the lunch bell sounded. She literally ran to Nancy's machine, grabbed her cloak and headed toward the stairs. The floor lady scolded, "Do not run!"

"How was your second day?" Mrs. Libby asked as she ladled a creamy soup with unidentified vegetables.

"I did not lose my cloak and I think I can find my way to my machine. Life is looking up," she laughed.

"After lunch you will lead the way back," Nancy suggested.

"If anyone is interested I will be giving piano lessons on Tuesday evenings for 5 cents per half hour and reading and writing lessons for 5 cents per half hour on Wednesday evenings."

Some of the girls murmured in their seats. "Believe me, if you did not pay for your lessons you would be disinclined to practice. Of course I would perfectly understand if you found an instructress who charged less."

Mrs. Libby quietly laughed in the kitchen as she heated up the dish water. The bell rang. "Nancy, follow me," Rachel instructed.

The mill did not appear to be as formidable, once Rachel was confident she could find her way to and from her machine and back home. She doubted she would ever find her way around the entire mill.

She spent the next few hours designing lesson plans in her head. The afternoon ran smoothly until the room grew dark and the lamps were lit. The smell was worse than the noise and the heat and the floating lint. "If I can survive the winter, there will be no lamps come summer," she tried to convince herself. As the bell rang she turned off her machine, calmly walked to Nancy's station and strolled home enjoying every gulp of the cold fresh air.

Silently she went into her room, changed into her pink and blue cotton dress and returned downstairs to the sitting room where she found two piano students and Mrs. Libby expectantly waiting. "You did not expect a washer woman to give piano lessons, did you?" she laughed. "First I will warm up with some scales," she demonstrated. An octave consists of eight notes. We will begin with the key of C. The octave begins with C and ends with C. C, D, E, F, G, A, B, C" she said aloud as she played each note.

"What happened to H?" Suzanne asked.

"I should have charged 10 cents per half hour," she thought. "Good question! How shall we learn if we do not ask questions?" She heard her grandfather say those words a thousand times. "There are only 7 notes you need to know A-G and then it repeats. This is an octave A to A," she stretched her hand to play both notes. "B to B, C to C and so forth."

"Why did you not begin with A when you played the scale? Why begin with C?" Mrs. Libby asked.

"Another good question! The white keys are called naturals. The black keys are called sharps and flats. The C scale is the only one that does not contain a sharp or a flat. Therefore it is the easiest to practice. This week's lesson is to practice the scale of C with first your right hand and then with your left. Now watch closely. We only have five fingers but eight notes. You play the first three notes with the first three fingers," she demonstrated, "then cross your thumb under your middle finger and continue to play the next five notes with all five fingers. Now you try."

Mrs. Libby laughed as she fumbled. "It is not as simple as it looks! I can practice during the day while you girls are at the mill. Suzanne, you try."

Suzanne was pleased when she did somewhat better. Dorothy played slowly but perfectly. "Excellent! It is better to play slowly, with good form and no mistakes than quickly and carelessly. Speed will naturally come with time. Our next assignment is to be able to identify the notes on the piano. Next week I will show you how to read the notes on paper. Suzanne, please play a D for me."

The Textile Mill

She hesitated, "If this is C then the next one is D, right?"

"Very good. Dorothy, please find A."

The music stopped, she collected three nickels, placed them in her apron pocket and she, her students and an audience of ten left to eat their supper in the dining room.

Each afternoon she briefly watched her students practice their scales and called out a random note for them to find. After their practice time she would play one song before dinner.

Rachel was terribly demoralized Saturday afternoon when she discovered that she would not receive her wages until next Saturday. She worried as she walked home in the cold, pouring rain. Saturday was the day the girls paid their rent. What was she to do? After supper she helped carry in some dirty dishes to the kitchen. "Mrs. Libby, there is an unfortunate situation I must discuss. It appears that I shall not be paid until next week."

"Everyone knows that, dear. I do hope you are not too disappointed."

"How shall I pay my rent?"

"Did your brother not tell you? Your grandfather paid for your first two weeks. He understood that your rent is due in advance for the upcoming week and you would not be paid until next week."

"Mrs. Libby, please make a pot of chamomile tea and I shall begin reading *The Last of the Mohicans*. Twenty girls, some with their sewing crowded into the sitting room.

Like a mother duck leading her ducklings, Mrs. Libby led her girls to the Second Congregational Church on Sunday morning and back to the boarding house. After Sunday dinner, Rachel put on her moccasins and took a walk with Dorothy, Suzanne, Nancy and six others to Saco Bay. How she missed being outdoors! She missed the freedom of walking to her grandparents' house for an errand or for a visit. She missed walking over the covered bridge to Eli's house. She even missed walking to the barn to call her father to supper. She never appreciated breathing the clear mountain air until she spent seventy-three hours suffocating on cotton lint. She survived her first week and she was determined to survive at least one entire year!

"Look at the boats!" she gasped as she surveyed the bay bustling with activity.

"They are called schooners," Dorothy corrected. "Those over there are unloading bales of cotton from Georgia and Alabama."

"These over here are unloading whale oil from New Bedford,"[3] Suzanne added.

Rachel tried not to appear shocked at the cussing and the fact they were working on a Sunday. Several of the men from the New Bedford schooner turned to stare at them and Dorothy boldly smiled at them.

"It is time to leave," Rachel suggested.

"What harm will it do just to talk?" Dorothy challenged. "We never get to talk to any men."

"Trust me, these are not the kind of men with whom ladies would wish to speak," she warned. They must be the men her father warned her about. "Let us head back. It will be getting dark soon and it will not be wise to be found near the docks at twilight." She quickly walked away with the others following closely behind.

It was bitterly cold one late November afternoon as Rachel returned to the boarding house after dark. The girls excitedly surrounded a small wooden chest in the sitting room. "This arrived by stage coach this afternoon," Mrs. Libby explained.

"Just don't stand there! Open it!" they cried excitedly.

"Nancy, we shall begin your lessons tonight," Rachel smiled as she held up three slates with chalk and the first two books of the McGuffey readers. There was a large tin of chamomile tea with Mrs. Libby's name on it. A newly-repaired quilt with new wool backing from Aunt Grace, and an extra wool blanket from her mother would keep her warm this winter. Sadie had packed an oil painting of Swans Falls that she had painted before Rachel was born. Her grandmother included a package of paper and six quills for her students. Her father had made her deer hide boots which went up to her shins. Inside one boot was a note from her mother warning her to wear them on rainy or snowy days or she would catch a cold standing in wet shoes all day.

The best treasure was the letters at the bottom of the chest which she quickly placed in her apron pocket. "Have my students practiced their piano lessons today?" she reminded. Suzanne and Dorothy took their turns at the piano. "I will practice double tomorrow," Mrs. Libby promised sheepishly.

Nancy was so excited about her first lesson she could hardly eat. "After supper we will sit at the writing table in my room," Rachel offered. "I think it will be wise if we simply start at the beginning and let you progress at your own pace. Each evening you may practice your penmanship on a slate."

Nancy was embarrassed that she would barely read at Level One. "Just as my piano students must begin with their scales, you must begin with the alphabet. When they learn to put the notes together they will play a song. When you learn to put the letters together, you will read a book. You must take one step at a time to arrive at your destination. Now you may practice your penmanship while I read my letters."

Dear Rachel,

Your grandfather and I are truly proud of you for wisely spending your spare moments teaching. I am enclosing the slates and soapstone you have requested. Your grandfather insisted that he buy you more paper and quills.

I hope your student progresses as quickly as Darian who is a bright boy and eager to learn. I will send you the last two books in the series.

I was thrilled to learn that the boarding house has a piano and you have begun giving piano lessons. Perhaps you may use the enclosed paper to draw the staff and to teach them how to read music. I regret to this day that I never learned.

We have ceased our afternoon walks because the weather is simply too cold. We had several inches of snow yesterday and Aunt Grace has also stopped walking down for her visits. I think I may ask Darian to take the carriage and bring her, for I miss her terribly.

Your grandfather is very upset that Zachary Taylor has won the election. He is convinced that the country will split in two. I may convince Abigail to drive her father to the general store for a visit someday this week. The change in scenery will be good for both of us.

Please be sure to write your mother at least once a week. She does worry so about you.

Your loving Grandmother,
Nana

Dear Rachel,
Danny and Emily have assured us that the boarding house is up to my standards. I have enclosed another blanket and quilt now that the nights are growing colder. It is better to have them and not need them, than to need them and not have them. Remember you can always use your cloak as an extra blanket.

Please wear your new boots to work. I know that they are not fashionable, but you must not work all day in wet shoes. Rachel smiled to herself. If her mother could see her at the mill wearing her old work dress and moccasins! *You are wise to drink chamomile tea in place of coffee. Please take good care of yourself.*

Love,
Mama

The Textile Mill

Dear Rachel,
Tomorrow Papa and Eli are taking Darian and me hunting. School is boring. I cannot wait until Darian will come with me next year.
Will you be coming home for Christmas?
Your dutiful brother,
Isaac

Rachel did not know how she would tell her brother that she intended to never return home.

XI

Life without Rachel

Isaac awoke before dawn that Saturday morning anticipating the exciting day ahead. His father was taking him hunting! As soon as he heard Jacob stirring he jumped out of bed and got dressed. By the time he ran down to the kitchen his mother had breakfast started and Eli had arrived.

"Danny said you may have this," Jacob handed Isaac a rifle.

After Eli rolled his eyes in disgust Jacob responded, "Not every man is destined to be a hunter. I respect your brother's decision. He will not be scaring off the deer by shooting and missing and he has given his gun to someone who will appreciate it. I think we should all be grateful," he winked at Isaac who was reverently holding his prized possession.

Joshua and Darian, who was bundled up from head to foot, arrived through the back door. "Nana was worried he would catch his death of cold and Darian was polite enough to respect her wishes," Joshua smiled.

"Of course we men will never tell if you choose to shed a few layers," Jacob laughed.

"Darian, where did you get your gun?" Eli asked.

"He is borrowing mine. I am too old to spend a day in the cold with nothing to show for my misery," Joshua shook his head. "We did a little target practice after I sighted in the gun. He is a natural."

"Isaac you will come with me and Darian will go with Eli," Jacob explained.

"I shall return to my heated office, gentlemen," Joshua waved as he headed out into the cold.

Once again Kate washed the breakfast dishes in silence. She had never before appreciated Rachel's pleasant chatter and laughter while doing morning chores. It would be another long and lonely morning. Perhaps Julia and the children would stop by to break up the monotony of the day. She sighed as she placed another dirty dish into the bucket of hot water.

The four entered their favorite hunting ground just as the sun was rising. Jacob with a talkative Isaac headed west up a hill while Eli led Darian to the east on level ground. "A good hunter needs three things – patience, silence and a steady hand. I fear my little brother has none of these," Eli muttered. They stopped in front of a large, forked pine tree. "This was Uncle Micah's favorite hunting spot." He gave Darian a boost. "If you need me I will be over there past a stand of birches." Eli silently entered the bush and disappeared from sight.

After an hour, Darian was bored, hungry and tired. He slowly and quietly shifted his weight and sighted his gun. America's trees were so big; its forests so vast!

To pass the time he pretended to be a sniper sitting on the roof of his cottage waiting for British soldiers guarding a shipment of Irish grain to pass. If he could shoot the soldiers without being seen or heard, he could return the grain to his village and save his family. He would sit there all day if he had to, but he would save his family.

A rustling of leaves broke the silence. The British were coming! He steadily held up his gun and patiently waited for the soldier to walk into in his line of fire. The unsuspecting soldier's head was in his cross hairs. Darian held his breath as he slowly squeezed the trigger.

As the sound of gunshot pierced the air, a six point buck fell to the ground and the kick back of the rifle knocked him out of the tree.

Eli came running through the woods and stopped short by the fallen animal. "I cannot believe it!"

Darian slowly stood up in a daze, "Neither can I." He could not believe how easy it was to kill.

The whole family gathered around the buck strung up on a tree by the barn.

"When Rachel comes home for Christmas we will have venison stew!" Isaac celebrated. He had been counting the days for his sister's return.

Jacob and Kate looked at each other wordlessly as Jacob slowly shook his head.

"Rachel is not coming home for Christmas," Eli explained. "She only has one day off. How could she possibly arrive and return in one day?"

Isaac turned to his parents, "That is not true. She is coming home."

"Son, I am afraid it is true."

"She is never coming home, is she?" he yelled, ran into the house and slammed the door.

"Eli, did you have to?" Jacob rebuked.

"You should have told him by now. When I was his age –"

Jacob put his hand up to demand silence.

Joshua knocked on Darian's bedroom door Sunday morning. "Breakfast is waiting for you," he invited.

"I am not hungry," he mumbled under the covers.

Joshua observed his red swollen eyes and surmised he had been crying. "Are you ill?" he asked with paternal concern.

"I do not feel well. Please tell Mrs. Miller that I will not be keeping the Sabbath with her today. I just want to be alone."

"Very well. Perhaps she and Mr. Miller will attend services together today." He left the room and went downstairs.

"Mother, Darian is not well and wishes to stay in bed. Perhaps the three of you can go to church this morning and I will stay home just in case he needs anything," Joshua offered.

"I knew he would catch a chill," Hannah fretted.

Joshua reentered Darian's room. "Mrs. Miller made you some tea," he placed the tea cup on the table by the bed as Darian feigned sleep. "It will make you feel better."

While the family attended church Joshua read the Scriptures in his office. He heard Darian quietly descend the back staircase and place the cup and saucer on the table. Suddenly he heard the cup smash against the wall as Darian sobbed bitterly. He opened the glass door to the cupboard and began smashing plates, bowls and cups as he cursed. When the smashing stopped, Joshua quickly arose and entered the room.

"You forgot a plate," Joshua threw it on the floor.

"I hate them all!" Darian screamed. "They all act like Rachel's dead. What do they know? One sister moves and it is the end of the world! They don't know what it's like to..."

"Too lose everyone you love? To lose your home and everything you own?" Joshua finished the sentence.

"Some of us know, Darian. Before I married Mrs. Pierce I had a wife, two children and a law practice down in Salem. I was away overnight on business and returned to discover I lost them and everything I owned in a fire. I thought I would go mad. I did more than break a set of dishes."

"You lost everything?"

"All I had left was God. It took me many years to learn that if you have God you have everything. I hope in time you will see that too. I still miss them. Although I am grateful for the life I have, I still wonder what my life would have been like if I had not lost them."

Grief takes time. Someday you will be grateful for the life you have now, but you will still miss your family. We are not trying to take your family's place. We are simply trying to give you a new home."

"What will I do about the dishes?" Darian stared down at the floor at the smashed blue and white willow ware.

"We will clean up the mess before they return. I do not wish to have Mr. Miller trip and fall."

"What will I tell them?"

"We will tell them the truth."

"How will they eat?"

"We have other dishes. Can you keep a secret? Mr. Miller bought those as a gift years ago. I heard Mrs. Miller say she thought they were a bit ostentatious. Of course she would never tell Mr. Miller that. Tomorrow we will escort her to the general store to let her buy some new dishes."

"That is not fair. You did not break the dishes."

"Life is not fair. It is not fair my first family died. It is not fair your family starved while the British did nothing."

"That is a strange thing for an Englishman to say."

"I am an American, not an Englishman," he corrected.

"Pierce is an English surname."

"My father was a Pierce. My mother was an O'Malley."

"You are an Irishman?"

"No, I am an American. Please do not hate the Millers. Mr. Miller's father wrote me letters of sympathy and encouragement and invited me to live with them when I had no place to go. But when I finally arrived, he had died."

"What did you do?"

"The rest of the family took me in."

"They took you in so now you take me in?" Darian asked.

"Yes, and I hope someday you will do the same for someone else. Grief takes a long time to overcome. The next time you feel rage, come to me first before you break something."

The carriage pulled up to the front of the house. Joshua and Darian went out to help Benjamin and Hannah out of the carriage. "We need to speak to you in the office," Joshua invited his in-laws. When all of them were seated at the conference table Joshua began, "After I lost my family years ago, I did many things which I now regret. This morning Darian's grief got the better of him."

"Mrs. Miller, I smashed your dishes because I was angry at Isaac for acting like a baby. His sister is not dead, she only moved away!"

Hannah put her hand on Darian's shoulder. "I have no concern about broken dishes for they are easily replaced.

Darian bit his lip and stared out the window.

"Have a seat," Jacob pointed to the settee in the sitting room. "Isaac, you must change your ways," he sternly warned his son. "There will be no more childish outbursts like last night. Do you understand me?"

"But Papa –"

"Do not interrupt me when I am speaking! You are forbidden to write anymore letters to your sister begging her to come home. You are upsetting Rachel and your mother. We all miss her, especially your mother. Rachel is a grown woman able to make her own decisions. You should write to say how proud you are of her.

How do you think Darian feels when you are carrying on like a child about your sister not coming home for Christmas?"

"Is it true he smashed Nana's dishes?"

"I would have done the same thing myself. Now begin to think of others before yourself. Think before you speak!"

"Yes, Papa."

"I must tell you that Abigail's reading circle is a wonderful idea. I cannot wait to begin Friday evening," Grace enthused over supper.

"Jacob I do not see how I will find the time. Winter may be a slow period for some, but not for me," Kate reminded her husband.

"Mama, I can help you get your medicines ready to sell at the general store," Isaac offered. "I know what to do. I watched you make infusions, tinctures, and poultices my whole life."

"I can read aloud while the two of you are busy with your herbs," Grace volunteered.

"I will agree to attend Friday evening," Kate conceded. "However I do not promise to attend every week."

Abigail spent all day Friday cleaning the house and baking a pound cake. Daniel and Emily, Eli and family, Grace, Jacob, Kate and Isaac, Reverend and Mrs. Hurd, Peter Evans and Mr. and Mrs. Weston all arrived promptly at 6:00 and filled the law office – the only room large enough to accommodate the crowd.

"James Fennimore Cooper is America's most celebrated novelist," Abigail began. "I have selected *The Last of the Mohicans* because it is based on the true story of Fort William Henry during the French and Indian War."

"Those French are not to be trusted," Grace warned.

"Certainly not the French at Fort William Henry," Abigail agreed. The young ladies at Fryeburg Academy never spoke out of turn when she was teaching.

"I understand that Mr. Cooper read Joseph Frye's account of the events and used those materials for his research. He wrote the novel ninety-one years after the actual events," Abigail continued.

"Who is Joseph Frye?" Isaac innocently asked.

"Who is Joseph Frye?" Grace repeated in disbelief. "Do these schools teach our children nothing?"

"Colonel Joseph Frye is the founder of our town. He was born in Andover, Massachusetts in 1712 and joined the militia to fight the French and the Indians. He served in

Acadia where he was obliged to assist in the transportation of the Acadian peasants from their homes and then burned their houses. He found this very distasteful."[1]

Darian recalled scenes of the British forcing Irish tenants out of their homes. He did not think he would like this Joseph Frye.

"In 1757 he was in the unfortunate capture of Fort William Henry by Montcalm. In the confusion on the attack upon the defenseless British and colonial troops, an Indian chief seized Col. Frye and led him into a secluded spot in the woods. In desperation he sprang upon the savage, overpowered him and killed him before fleeing into the thick wood to elude the Indians. After wandering for several days living on whortleberries, he reached Fort Edwards and joined his suffering companions."[2]

"I remember when I was a child that he would keep a fast each year in memory of his suffering from insects and lack of food," Benjamin added. "After this war he petitioned the Royal Government for a land grant as reward for his loyal service. The town was called Pequawket back then. During the Revolutionary War he was appointed to command forces in Falmouth. Today we call it Portland."

"Papa, you personally knew Joseph Frye?" Abigail asked with interest.

"When I was a child, he was an elderly man. He owned a store and sometimes my father would take me to the store where we would exchange pleasantries."

"Did Mr. Frye really kill Indians?" Isaac asked. Maybe this book would not be so boring after all.

"Son, war is a terrible thing. Sometimes men are forced into situations which they would never choose," Jacob solemnly explained.

"Perhaps this may not be the most suitable literary selection for the young ones," Daniel suggested.

"This book sounds interesting–not like the boring stuff we have to read in school," Isaac argued.

"I believe this novel is neither suitable for the children nor the women folk," Hannah continued.

"Mama, women and children are impacted by war as well. Although war may not be pleasant to think about, it is a reality. Pretending it does not exist will not cease its existence."

"Hannah, dear there was a famous Indian battle right here in Fryeburg," Benjamin reminded.

"There was an Indian battle here?" Isaac asked incredulously? "In Fryeburg?"

"Do these children know any history?" Grace asked again in exasperation.

"Did you in fight in the battle, Grandpa?" Isaac asked.

Benjamin laughed, "No, this battle was 124 years ago back in 1725. Fryeburg was not yet a town. It happened on the pond we now call Lovewell Pond named after Captain John Lovewell who led the battle."

"Did you ever see an Indian?" Isaac asked.

"When I was a boy some Indians would visit Mr. Dresser in town. One afternoon my father and my brother Micah went over there and I saw some Indian children in the yard. But I was too shy to talk to them. My father always said if you respect them, they would respect us. But I think my mother was afraid of them."

"I do not know about your Joseph Frye but I think I would like to read this book," Darian added enthusiastically.

"May I suggest a novel by Charles Dickens?" Hannah offered.

"Hannah, I will gladly read *Nicholas Nickleby* to Darian each morning," Benjamin volunteered. "This will provide him with the opportunity to compare the writings of an American author with a British one."

Hannah lost the argument. The group would read *The Last of the Mohicans*.

Life without Rachel

"Good morning, Grandpa!" Eli greeted as he entered the kitchen where Benjamin was reading his newspaper, Hannah was sewing and Darian was writing in his copy book. "The thermometer read twenty-five below zero again this morning. Julia kept the girls home from school because she was afraid they would get frost bite. However she was not afraid that Davy would get frost bite if I brought him to the farm," he laughed.

"Well, the farm is much closer than the school," Benjamin logically reasoned.

"Where is Davy now?"

"He is spending the morning 'helping' his grandfather. He is certainly a hand full!"

"Like father, like son," Hannah mused. "I remember you being a handful." Darian put down his quill and looked up in interest. "At least Davy does not have a younger brother to tease."

"Was I really that bad?"

"Yes!" his grandparent emphatically replied in unison. Darian laughed out loud.

"It took three of us – Abigail, your mother and me to keep you out of mischief. Davy just needs someone to play with."

"I can play with him," Darian offered. "I can read books to him and teach him his letters. I watched my little brother all the time."

"I believe spending an hour or two after lunch may be beneficial to both boys," Hannah suggested.

"So Grandpa, what do you think of President Taylor?"

"Benjamin, I know how much you enjoy Eli's visits. Perhaps the two of you would like to discuss politics in the front parlor."

Benjamin slowly rose to his feet. "The country cannot continue divided like this. I fear that during your lifetime there shall be a civil war."

The next day Joshua and Darian shook the snow off of their hats before entering Evan's General Store. "Good morning, sir," Joshua greeted. "Has Mrs. Miller's new china arrived?"

"Yes, indeed." Peter took one ivory plate rimmed with gold out of the straw in a carefully packed crate. "I took the liberty of unpacking it to inspect for any breakage. Mr. Pierce and Mr. Flynn, I believe you have made a fine choice, a simple but elegant pattern that will please her Quaker taste."

"Mrs. Miller would also like some brown woolen fabric for a coat. She insists that Thaddeus' hand me down is not warm enough."

"Well I think our Irish hunter deserves a warm winter coat, do you not?" Mr. Evans smiled. Some of the older gentlemen in the store concurred.

Ever since Darian had shot the buck two months ago, strangers would stop him on the street to congratulate him and then reminisce about their first buck. Fryeburg took their hunting seriously.

"Widow Miller received a package. Darian, would you be able to deliver it to her?" Mr. Evans asked.

"Yes, sir."

"Thank you Darian," Grace excitedly opened her package.

"What is it, Aunt Grace?" Eli asked curiously as he stared at the leather bond journal."

"There is no writing in it," Darian observed.

"Not yet but there will be," she promised. "I am going to write the history of Fryeburg. Someone must teach this generation about their town." She took her journal, sat at her mother's oak writing desk, dipped her quill into the ink and began.

The Fryeburg Chronicles
By Grace Peabody Miller
February 14, 1849

"How was school today?" Kate asked her son as he entered the kitchen.

"It was boring as usual," he replied. "I would much rather help you set up your herbs for Mr. Evans' store. I do not see how people are expected to learn while sitting still with their hands folded. God created people to move and hands to do useful things!"

Kate laughed and tousled his curly, dark brown hair. "I could not have said it better myself! I have been waiting for you to return."

"You have?"

"I have been thinking about Mr. Evans' new apothecary all week and I simply do not know where to begin. Mrs. Evans only knows the most basic knowledge about remedies and Mr. Evans knows less. He is all excited that his son-in-law built him an apothecary cabinet filled with little drawers and now he wants to fill them. There must be a proper method of displaying and dispensing them!"

"All the dried leaves can be safely stored in the drawers away from the light. It should be in alphabetical order as to find each item quickly. The syrups and tinctures can be stored in stoneware crocks.

I can write the information on each herb, its properties and uses."

Kate looked at her son in surprise.

"Mama, I spent my whole life listening to you and Rachel. Peppermint tea is for an upset stomach, clove oil is for a tooth ache, a poultice of yarrow is for infected wounds, and mullein tea is for congested lungs."

For the first time since her daughter left home, Kate laughed in delight.

"If you can convince Papa to let me stay home from school I could help you with all of this and we would be done in no time," Isaac suggested.

"There were days when Eli and Daniel stayed home to help your papa. I cannot think that he would object to you helping me. After all God made people to move and hands to be busy," she smiled tenderly.

One Saturday morning in mid-March Hannah and Grace were admiring Mr. Evans new apothecary. "That young Isaac is quite a boy. He wrote out all of these labels and directions. You must be very proud of him, Mrs. Miller."

"I am proud of all of my grandchildren," she replied.

Suddenly the door flung open. Isaac announced to all within earshot. "The sap is running. Nana, can Darian come and help?"

"May Darian come and help?" Hannah corrected.

"Yes Mam. Well can he? Uncle Joshua has declared it a holiday and is changing into his work clothes."

"I am certain your father and Eli could use all the help they can get. Does Ireland have maple trees, Darian?"

"No Mam," he was not going to admit that he had no idea what everyone was talking about.

Joshua drove the boys over to the farm in a wagon filled with snowshoes, wooden buckets, braces, bits and spiels where he met Eli and his entire family similarly prepared and ready to go.

"We will meet the others at the sugar house," Jacob explained. Twenty years ago Uncle Micah and Jacob had built a three sided out building in a clearing by a maple grove. It was here that friends and neighbors poured their sap into large iron kettles over open flames. The men and boys would venture into the woods with their buckets while the women and girls kept watchful eyes on the sap cooking down into syrup and sugar.

Darian wordlessly observed Joshua drill small holes into trees and place spiels into the holes. His job was to hang the bucket under the spiel as Joshua proceeded to the next hole. To his amazement a clear liquid began pouring into the bucket. "I remember taking Thaddeus with me every spring," he reminisced.

"How did this liquid turn into sugar?" Darian wondered as Eli drove a wagon holding several empty barrels. Darian carried the buckets of sap to Eli who emptied them into the barrel. Darian could hear Isaac talking excitedly to Daniel just over the hill. They continued working until nightfall when Eli arrived with an empty wagon.

"I thought you might like a lift back to the sugar house," Eli offered.

"We accept your offer with gratitude," Joshua responded wearily. Darian said nothing as he watched Joshua's hand tremble with fatigue.

The fires were warm and the air smelled sweet as Darian warmed himself by one of the fires. It was like a party! Thirty to forty people were eating bread and cheese and drinking cider; younger children were running and laughing. Off to the side Sadie had set up her easel as she painted the scene before her.

"Have you ever tried leather britches before?" Emily asked Darian.

"No Mam." He was thankful he wore woolen britches.

She ladled thick, amber liquid upon some snow, rolled it up with a wooden spoon and handed it to him. "Try some leather britches."

He tasted the sweet confection and thought, "In America the trees make candy!"

XII

The Sawyer

The first Saturday in May Darian and Isaac hopped on the back of one of Uncle Micah's huge draft horses and left to spend the day at Daniel's saw mill. Darian felt the sunshine on his straw hat and a warm breeze on his face as they traveled through the village and headed to the sawmill deep into the woods near the rushing Saco River.

Emily wiped her hands on her apron as she left the house to greet them. "Good morning!"

"Mama gave you some loaves of bread and a crock of butter," Isaac handed her a linen sack before he slid off the horse. "She thought you might need some help with the chores since this is Danny's busy season." What he did not say was since you do not have your own children to help with the chores. That was a topic which the family never discussed.

The boys brought in four armfuls of kindling, filling the wood box by the black cook stove. The kitchen had an indoor hand pump which pumped deliciously cold water into a large soapstone sink. Shelves above the sink held an assortment of salt glaze mixing bowls and pitchers. A large pine cupboard painted dark red was filled with mugs, bowls, plates, teapots and sugar bowls. There was no fancy china like Darian had seen at the other Miller homes. A small pantry filled with cooking utensils, rolling pins, bins of flour, oatmeal and rice connected the kitchen to the woodshed. An oval oak table and chairs were placed by the window with a view of the river. Red and white checked gingham curtains and a braided rug were the only adornments of this utilitarian room.

There was no fancy dining room. The large front room contained a long, pine trestle table covered with fabrics and sewing projects. Emily was a talented seamstress who sewed clothing for a growing clientele and frugally used the remnants to make clothing for the less fortunate. A maple bookcase was filled with leather bound books of all sizes. Several walnut chairs formed a semicircle around a massive parlor stove. Small tables with oil lamps were interspersed between the chairs. A ladder led to a loft; off to the side was a small but tidy bedroom.

Emily noticed Darian eyeing the loaves of bread. "I was about to take a break from my sewing. Would you two boys like to have some bread and apple butter? Dinner is still a few hours away." For the first time since he arrived in America Darian felt at home.

"Darian, I have more fabric than I know what to do with, are you in need of any clothing?"

"No, mam. Mrs. Miller found another trunk of Thaddeus' old clothes," he replied.

"I insist you call me Emily. If you are wearing Thaddeus' hand me downs, you will be the best dressed lad in Fryeburg.

Danny might need some help. Some of the seasonal help have returned to their farms."

Daniel Miller was the most respected employer in town and there was a waiting list of men eager to work for him. First he paid higher than average wages for he recognized that it was hard and dangerous work. Secondly he never required his men to do a job that he was not willing to do himself. In addition to the wages, he provided a comfortable bunk house for those who could not travel in the winter. He respected the farmers who were in his employ from post-harvest to pre- planting season and understood that the farms were their first priority. His year round employees were treated like members of an extended family.

However he was strict. Smoking tobacco was strictly forbidden because of the fire hazard. More than one man was fired immediately for breaking this infraction. Chewing tobacco was also forbidden since a former employee spat a wad which stained several boards of oak that were due to be delivered that afternoon.

No one dared to drink on the job since George Stevens' accident eight years ago. Each November Daniel would carefully select the needed timbers and marked them with red paint. Some lumber mills grumbled of nepotism for his relative Sadie Miller let him have first choice. Daniel and his crew would spend the winters chopping down their trees. After cutting off the branches, a team of oxen would drag the timbers to the shore of the frozen Saco River waiting for the spring melt.

River conditions and timing were crucial to a lumber drive. Again Daniel had an advantage. Because his land was adjacent to Sadie's, he needed to transport his logs a short distance saving transportation costs and valuable time. The lumber drive was the most dangerous part of the logging industry with men balancing on logs while pushing other logs with long pikes on the icy river. It was at unpredictable log jams where some men lost their lives.

George Stevens, the most experienced and acclaimed river jack in the Saco River valley, was perhaps overly confident of his skills. He did not fear that the half jug of whiskey he had consumed the previous evening would impair his balance or judgment. Five minutes into the drive George lost his balance, hitting his head on the log before falling into the river. To everyone's horror Daniel dove into the icy waters, grabbed the unconscious man and kept his head above the water before the two of them were swept by the current.

They were rescued a half a mile down river with Daniel suffering from hypothermia and George with a broken leg and crushed left hand. Emily took the sleigh to fetch Dr. Barrows who set George's broken leg; she tenderly nursed him for weeks afterward. His days of working in the woods were sadly over. Mrs. Stevens who was expecting their fourth child was distraught with the prospects of her unemployable husband. It was then Daniel hired him as the cook and handy man of the mill. From that day forward Daniel's employees never drank a drop while working.

Daniel's modest and quiet home was a contrast to his large and bustling saw mill. Darian was fascinated by the huge water wheel which powered the saws inside the mill.

"This is all new. This is called an overshot wheel," Isaac explained with self-importance. "Originally we had an undershot wheel where the river simply flowed under the wheel, driving the wheel. It worked great in the spring but was rather unreliable in August. Danny says it was inefficient. Grandpa bought him some books on water power and he spent two years, studying and drawing pictures before he expanded his mill.

His crew built this wooden sluice way almost thirty feet high which brings the water flow to the top of the wheel. The water fills the buckets into the wheel. As the buckets fill, the weight of the water starts to turn the wheel. The water spills out of the bucket on the down side into a spillway leading back to the river. Since the wheel itself is set above the spillway, the water never slows down the speed of the wheel. They had to construct a small dam upriver, a millpond, sluice gate and a spillway. Danny says it was worth the time and expense because now the mill is more than twice as efficient as the old way.[1]"

The boys found Daniel in the barn assisting the local cooper. "I have an order for a dozen barrels from Evans' General Store that needs to be completed right away."

"For liquids or dry goods?" Daniel asked knowing that white oak and ash were the best woods for holding liquids.

"Dry goods."

"Most of my white oak is green. However I have plenty of seasoned maple, ash, hickory and chestnut. Mr. Stevens will show you." An older man with a limp and deformed hand came out to help.

Spruce was used primarily for framing barns and in building bridges.[2] "I need two spruce timbers," a rugged farmer stated sheepishly. "I know you are working on Walker's Bridge and I hoped you would have some extra. I told my son, measure twice, cut once!"

"I think I can help you out. Do you need some oak for the trunnels?"

"I might as well since I am here," he grumbled.

Another farmer wanted some cedar to build fence posts.[3] As Daniel was writing up a receipt he noticed Isaac and Darian and smiled, "Would you boys please get the cedar into the wagon?"

Two wagons pulled in. "I have this," Daniel's brother-in-law Josiah Walker stated. "Good morning. Are you here to pick up your pine?"

"This is a busy place," Darian observed.

"If you think this is busy you should go on fire wood deliveries in the fall. Sometimes I help out," Isaac bragged.

"America sure has a lot of trees!" Darian stated as he looked around.

"Not only does America have lots of trees it has many kinds of trees," Daniel added. "The good Lord created different trees for different jobs. Coopers need certain woods for barrels. White oak and ash are the best to hold liquids. Maple, oak, ash, hickory and chestnut make good barrels for holding dry goods. Pine, birch and maple are ideal for making baskets, bowls, spoons, and boxes.[4] Tanners need hemlock.

Because cedar is resistant to rot, they make good fence posts and coffins.[5]

Pine is considered the prince of the forests because it has more practical uses than any other tree. It is light in weight and does not decay easily. It is first choice in covering barns and bridges. Birch is also perfect material for both lye-ash and charcoal."[6]

"Lye ash is used for soap making," Isaac explained.

"Chandlers and coopers are my biggest customers for birch. Because oak is the strongest of the woods, it is used for framing houses and barns and making trunnels. It is also long burning and is used for firewood. Spruce and ash can also be used for timber frames but the pegs must always be oak."

"Trees are like people. Different people have different jobs to do," Isaac explained philosophically.

"How can you tell the different trees apart?" Darian asked as he survey the lumber neatly stacked.

"That is easy once you spend a lot of time with them," Daniel laughed. "Could you sweep the saw dust out of the barn?" Daniel left the boys when two more wagons pulled up and returned when the boys were done.

"Could you help Mr. Stevens load my wagon with those cedar shingles?" he pointed to the neatly stacked piles near the shaving horse. Then cart the load over to Mr. Page's tannery and give him this invoice of the hemlock bark I delivered last week. George is needed here to make lunch and I need the wagon returned for another delivery this afternoon.

Darian, have you ever driven a team and wagon?"

He shook his head in embarrassment.

"Would you like to learn? Isaac will show you. It is an important skill for a man to have. Farmers make good money in the off season carting goods to and from Portland."

From the corner of his eye he spied the blackest boy he had ever seen hiding behind a stack of wood. "Look!" he pointed.

"I do not see anything," Isaac lied.

"Over there. There is a black boy. Now he ran behind those trees."

"I believe it is time to take Darian into our confidences," Daniel, who would never lie, conceded. "You see I export more than lumber," he placed his rough hand on the boy's slender shoulder.

"Mrs. Miller told me America has slaves from Africa. Is he a slave?"

"Not anymore," Daniel grinned. "This is a secret."

"It is a poorly kept secret," George laughed as he threw a bundle of shingles in the wagon. "Half the town of Fryeburg knows about it and the other half suspects."

"My father did this as a young boy back in '06."

Darian tried to imagine the soft spoken farmer with gray, curly hair as a young boy smuggling slaves down the river.

"It was my grandparents who planned and organized a chain of safe houses from Philadelphia to here and on to Canada."

Darian stood silent in disbelief. The dignified, elderly gentleman who read his books and newspapers and the kind, old lady who read her Bible were smugglers!

"We have never been caught yet," Isaac bragged.

"You mean I have never been caught yet," Daniel corrected.

"I will take over when you are old," Isaac informed him.

"Come here, son. You are among friends," Daniel beckoned the frightened boy. "They will take you to my house where you can eat and rest."

The boy timidly followed Isaac and Darian up the front steps into the large front room of the house.

"Welcome," Emily greeted. "I have some clothes for you. Winters are cold up in Canada. This great coat may be large for you today, but it will last several years. I will warm some water for you on the stove. Here is some soap and clean clothes. You may bathe with privacy in the pantry. I must burn your old clothes and destroy any evidence of your visit." Emily was too polite to say she must destroy any lice or vermin.

"If anyone is looking for you, they are searching for a boy in a ragged, white linen shirt and blue britches. But you will be dressed in a fine, red cotton shirt and brown trousers," Isaac explained.

"Now go get washed and changed and I will have soup and bread ready for lunch"

It occurred to Darian that the loaves and butter so expertly prepared by Isaac's mother was designated for this visitor and not for him. He felt compassion for this boy alone and far from home.

The three boys mutely ate their lunch as Emily burned the old clothes in the cook stove. Their guest nervously scanned the river. Darian had almost forgotten how hungry he had been the year before. Now he took for granted that there would be food at the next meal.

"May I suggest a rest after your all night journey?" Emily led him to the ladder to the loft.

Darian would have been afraid to walk through the woods alone all night. After all America had some very strange animals.

"George loaded the wagon all by himself," Daniel entered the house mildly annoyed. "Did you forget about the shingles?" Darian indeed had forgotten. "Isaac, show our guest the trap door under the bed up there. I built a false floor so people could disappear if they needed to. We never had need of it yet," he assured. "You will stay here a few days and then I will take you to the next house with a wagon load of potash. It will be a bumpy ride, but it will be better than walking."

Now Darian understood how natural it was for Thaddeus to bring home an orphan. His grandparents took him in, fed, clothed him and taught him to read. The family simply reacted as if unexpected visitors were a common occurrence. Americans were a generous people.

XIII

The Fight

Hannah had insisted on making Darian a new suit of clothes for his first day of school at the stone school house in the Village. "Could I just stay home and study with you for another year?" he pleaded with Hannah at breakfast.

"You know just as much as any other Fryeburg lad your age. You are ready for school," Benjamin pronounced. Darian knew it would be futile to argue.

"It appears that you shall not be walking alone to school," Hannah smiled as she watched her grandson and great grandchildren approach their kitchen door.

Davy ran in first. "Papa gave me a pen knife to trim my quills," he excitedly showed Darian.

"Good morning, Nana, Grandpa," Victoria greeted. "Mama made Becky and me matching dresses."

"You both look lovely today," Hannah agreed.

Isaac rolled his eyes. "Darian, I thought we could pick you up on our way to school each morning. It will be good to have another boy to walk with."

"I am a boy!" Davy protested.

"David, I believe Isaac meant another boy his age," Benjamin corrected. "You know how much you like to play with your friend, Monroe Quint. Well Isaac likes being with Darian because they are friends."

The Fight

"Do you have everything – slate, chalk, quill, copy book, lunch?" Hannah asked anxiously. "Run along. You do not want to be late for school."

"Nana, will you wave to me at the front window?" Davy asked.

"I cannot wave to you as long as you are standing in my kitchen," she laughed.

Darian took a deep breath and followed the others out the door. True to her word, Hannah was standing in the front window waving to all of them as they turned onto Main Street. She stood watching as they crossed the road and entered the school yard.

"Monroe," Davy ran over to his friend. "My grandfather made me this wooden top," he proudly pulled it out of his jacket pocket. "See?" he spun it on the smooth granite step.

A hand unexpectedly jerked the toy away.

"Hey! Give that back! That is my toy!" Davy yelled indignantly to the thirteen- year-old thief.

"Oh yeah. Who is going to make me?" he sneered.

"I am!" Darian grabbed the top from the surprised teenager.

"This school is for Americans and not for the Irish!" he called over his shoulder as he glumly walked away with his hands in his pockets.

"That was very brave of you," Victoria flattered.

"That was very brave or very stupid," Becky shook her head. "Everyone stays away from Henry Johnson. He is a bully."

"My father always told me a man has to stand up for himself," Darian replied with anger smoldering in his eyes. "I am not afraid of Henry Johnson. He should be afraid of me!" he told the admiring circle of students.

Miss Chandler, the school mistress, appeared at the door ringing her bell. Instantly the children divided into two lines, girls in one, boys in another, and lined up according to age. This put Darian directly in front of Henry.

"My father says all the Irish are a bunch of drunks," Henry sneered.

"That's funny coming from the town drunk!" Darian calmly replied. The children howled with laughter.

Miss Chandler frowned. "Ladies first," she called. The girls silently entered the school, hung their shawls on the pegs on the wall and took their seats on the right side of the classroom. They were followed by the boys who took off their straw hats, hung their jackets and sat on the left. Students were grouped by their levels in the McGuffey Reader. Henry sat with much younger boys who read from Level 2. Darian sat next to Isaac who read from Level 5.

"Mr. Flynn," Miss Chandler called.

Darian quickly stood up, "Yes, mam." Henry turned around and smirked.

"It is important that my scholars sit according to their levels and not with their friends."

"Yes, mam. I am half way through Level 5 and Mr. Miller advised me to take my seat with the Level 5 boys and not Level 6."

"Is that so," she said skeptically. "Please open your book to page 247 and read."

Darian effortlessly read *"Come," said Squeers, "let's go to the schoolroom; and lend me a hand with my school coat, will you?"*

Nicholas assisted his master to put on an old fustian shooting jacket, which he took down from a peg in the passage; and Squeers, arming himself with his cane, led the way across a yard to a door in the rear of the house.

"There," said the schoolmaster, as they stepped in together; "this is our shop, Nickleby."

It was such a crowded scene, and there were so many objects to attract attention, that at first Nicholas stared about him, really without seeing anything at all. By degrees, however, the place resolved itself into a bare and dirty room with a couple of windows, whereof a tenth part might be of glass, the remainder being stopped up with old copy books and paper.

"There were a couple of long, old, rickety desks, cut and notched, and inked and damaged in every possible way ; *two or three forms, a detached desk for Squeers, and another for his assistant. The ceiling was supported like that of a barn, by crossbeams and rafters, and the walls were so stained and discolored that it was impossible to tell whether they had ever been touched by paint or whitewash.*

Pale and haggard faces, lank and bony figures, children with the countenances of old men, deformities with irons upon their limbs, boys of stunted growth, and the others whose long, meager legs would hardly bear their stooping bodies, all crowded on the view together. There were little faces which should have been handsome, darkened with the scowl of sullen, dogged suffering; there was childhood with the light of its eye quenched, its beauty gone, and its helplessness alone remaining."

"Well done, young man," she smiled. "Do you enjoy reading?"

"Yes, mam. This is an excerpt from *Nicholas Nickleby*. Charles Dickens is one of my favorite authors although Mr. Miller says Dickens over uses semi colons. I vividly remember reading this scene; that was the moment I realized that there are poor hungry English children as well as Irish children. *Last of the Mohicans* is also a favorite. Mrs. Miller thought the violence was not proper for children to read. She is a Quaker you know and very sensitive to these matters."

"Very well. Please take your seat. As I begin to work with the younger students, I would like the rest of you to take out your copy books and copy what I have written on the board." Miss Chandler found Darian's penmanship to be acceptable. Although adding and subtracting came easily to him, he regretted not memorizing his multiplication tables.

Darian was hungry and the sun was not yet overhead; he had at least an hour before noon. Mercifully the hour passed and Miss Chandler declared it lunch time. The girls took their lunch pails and proceeded outside in an orderly fashion to enjoy the remaining days of the waning autumn. Next the boys vacated the classroom in semi chaos.

The girls were playing graces. Victoria had her mother's old embroidery hoop with green and pink ribbons tied to it. She placed two sticks through it and tossed it into the air with the ribbons gracefully flowing behind. Becky quickly caught it with her two sticks and threw it to a nearby playmate.

"Darian, do you want to play marbles with us?" the younger boys invited as they drew a circle in the dirt with a stick.

He was flattered by the attention. "I am sorry but I do not own any marbles."

"You can play with mine," someone offered.

"Please play with us," they pleaded.

Darian realized that they were not so much seeking a playmate as a protector. "I think I would like to stand and watch," he crossed his arms as he stood as a shield between them and their tormentor.

Henry walked over to him, "My father says Catholics are going to hell."

The boys stopped their game and looked up in horror.

"Well I guess you will be in good company then," Darian replied nonplussed.

Even the girls giggled at that response. Henry swore and kicked a stone into the circle. Darian did not react and ignored the seething boy standing two feet behind him.

The pupils groaned when Miss Chandler rang her bell announcing the end of lunch. The girls quickly lined up and entered the school. The young school mistress stepped outside to supervise the boys as they fell into formation.

Davy could not concentrate on his spelling words as he worried if Henry would follow him home and steal his top. He knew he was safe as far as the farm because Isaac would be with him. What if Henry followed him from the farm over Weston's Bridge to his house? He decided to stay at the farm with his father until he was certain Henry was gone.

But who would walk Monroe home? Would his friend be safe? Davy never realized that school could be so complicated.

Miss Chandler dismissed the class and once again the girls lined up to exit first and the boys followed. To Davy's relief Monroe was a member of a large group heading toward the general store. There should be safety in numbers. Davy accompanied his sisters, Isaac and Darian and began to cross the road when Henry caught up with them.

"I bet you think you are pretty smart for an Irishman!"

"No, I think you are pretty stupid for an American."

Isaac could not stop himself from laughing.

"What's so funny?" Henry turned to Isaac and made a fist. He never saw Darian's fist as it connected to his jaw. He staggered and fell into the road with a yelp followed by a string of curse words.

"You leave my friends alone or the next time I will break more than your jaw!" Darian threatened. Davy had already run into the front door of his great grandfather's house yelling, "Help! He's going to kill all of us!"

Joshua and a client ran out of the office, Abigail hurried from the kitchen, Benjamin put down his newspaper and Hannah helped him to his feet.

"Who is going to kill you?" Joshua demanded.

"We are fine, Uncle Joshua. Darian will protect us. He is very brave," Victoria added.

"If I was a boy, I would have punched Henry Johnson years ago," Becky looked accusingly at Isaac as he entered the front door with Darian.

"Just a school yard scuffle," Joshua shook his head and he returned to his office.

"Darian, were you in a fight on your first day of school?" Hannah asked incredulously.

He stood there silently rubbing his right fist.

"You better tell Nana. She is going to hear about it anyway," Isaac warned.

"Henry Johnson is the biggest bully at school and Miss Chandler does not even try to stop him," Victoria began indignantly. "He is always picking on the younger children. The first thing this morning Henry grabbed Davy's top and would not give it back. Darian grabbed it from him and returned it. Then Henry spent the rest of the day calling Darian bad names, but Darian just ignored him. On the way home Henry was going to punch Isaac, so Darian punched Henry first."

Hannah sighed, "Jesus told us to turn the other cheek."

"Do you mean I am supposed to hit him twice?"

Once again Isaac could not stop himself from laughing.

"Isaac, you are not helping the situation," Benjamin scolded his grandson. "I think it will be best if you children run along home. I trust there are no killers lurking in the bushes," he chuckled.

Just to be safe the children exited from the back door and ran through the field to avoid being seen from the street.

"Darian, violence is not a solution," Hannah began. "Did St. Patrick strike his captors?"

Benjamin disagreed, "If the teacher was doing her job in supervising and disciplining her pupils this unfortunate event would not have occurred. I thank you Darian for defending your family. A man needs to protect women and children."

Darian felt proud for Mr. Miller called him a man and loved because Mr. Miller called the family "your family". Perhaps he had a family to love and protect.

"Darian tonight you will go to bed without your supper," Hannah pronounced.

The Fight

Eli entered through the back door, "Davy told me what you did in school today. Thank you for watching out for my children when I was not there."

Hannah stood up abruptly, "Gentlemen, if you will please excuse me I shall see if we have received any mail. I am expecting a letter from Rachel." She put on her bonnet, wrapped her woolen shawl around her shoulders and grabbed her cane. "Men," she muttered under her breath as she left through the front door.

As Daniel and Emily headed down the main street in their wagon, Emily spotted Hannah in the distance approaching Evans' General Store. "There is your grandmother," she pointed.

"Well, it is a beautiful afternoon for a walk as well as a ride," he smiled at his wife. Daniel was in good spirits for he had been paid in cash by the cooper and the tanner. Mr. Evans had given him a generous credit at the store for the cedar shingles he had delivered last week. Today he would buy Emily as much fabric and ribbons she needed to sew during the winter.

When Hannah entered the store she heard a man cursing loudly to a small audience. "Our schools are for Americans not the Irish! If we let the Irish in before you know it we will be letting in Negroes. All the Irish are good for is drinking and fighting. That Irish boy beat up my son for no reason. Do you think that good for nothing child will be punished? You can bet that Judge Miller will protect him. That boy is out of control. They can't even make him go to church on Sunday."

"Mr. Johnson," Hannah boldly approached the intoxicated man. "I can excuse your dim witted son for his ignorance because he has not been taught any better at home. The acorn does not fall far from the tree. Sir, what is your excuse? I am certain your dear mother raised you better than this."

Mr. Evans came running over to intervene. "Mrs. Miller, you have received a letter from your granddaughter. Come with me and I will get it for you."

"You are a disgrace! Do you want to end up like your father? Maybe if you spent more time in church and less time in the taverns…"

"See here, Mrs. Miller."

"Do not speak impertinently to me, young man," she waved her cane at him.

He took a large step back and tripped over a wooden crate of apples.

"That boy of yours broke my son's jaw! He should be in jail!" he screamed as Daniel and Emily entered the store.

"If that imbecile of yours comes anywhere near my great grandchildren I will break more than his jaw," she threatened.

"Nana!" Daniel came running over. "Nana let me take you home. You should not get yourself so upset. Mr. Johnson, let me help you up, sir."

Daniel's offer was met with a barrage of cursing and verbal abuse against the entire Miller clan. Daniel blushed at the thought of his grandmother hearing such language. He gently took Hannah's arm, "Let me take you home," he spoke softly.

"I will not be leaving without my mail," she insisted.

Mr. Evans handed her the letter. "Thank you. Mr. Evans, you really should be more discerning with whom you choose to do business. But this is what happens when you sell rum and whisky to the likes of him." She turned around with a swish of her petticoats, held her head high, took her grandson's arm and waltzed out of the establishment. If only Grace had been there to witness the scene, she would have been amused by her sister-in-law.

Hannah was filled with remorse. "Do not speak of this to your grandfather," she warned.

"You know he is going to hear about it. He should hear it from you," he explained.

"Mrs. Miller, are you not well? You are not yourself," Emily asked sweetly.

The Fight

"Perhaps I need a rest," she suggested as Daniel helped her into his wagon.

Benjamin spied the wagon and opened the back door. Daniel assisted his pale and trembling grandmother up the stairs.

"Hannah, dear what happened? What is wrong?" Benjamin gasped.

"Mama?" Abigail took her mother's arm and led her to her favorite chair in the parlor.

"Should I get my mother?" Eli offered.

"Should I run and get Dr. Barrows?" Darian asked in concern.

"All I need is a cup of chamomile tea and a rest," she sighed deeply.

"Daniel, what happened?" Benjamin asked.

"Mr. Johnson spoke some unkind words."

Mr. Evans was knocking at the front door and Eli let him in. "Mrs. Miller, I cannot tell you how sorry I am about this whole upsetting incident! Believe me neither Mr. Johnson nor his unruly son will ever enter my store again."

"Will someone please tell me what happened?" Benjamin demanded.

"Mr. Johnson was rudely rehashing a school boys' altercation and Mrs. Miller simply came to Darian's defense."

"One must defend one's family," Hannah justified her behavior.

Darian swallowed the lump his throat as Hannah called him family.

"Nana, you always told us that violence begets more violence and we should turn the other cheek," Daniel reminded.

"Danny, only girls back away from a fight," Eli argued. "A man stands up and fights."

"It takes a bigger man to walk away from a fight than to start one," Daniel snapped.

"Did you not defend our grandmother?" Eli accused.

"Your brother handled the situation like a perfect gentleman and calmly took his grandmother home," Mr. Evans explained.

Eli rolled his eyes. Daniel gave his older brother a dirty look.

"I am very confused," Darian confessed. "Fighting is good. Fighting is bad. Turn the other cheek. Stand up and defend your family. What am I supposed to think?"

"I think there will be two of you going to bed without your suppers," Benjamin laughed.

XIV

Journey Home

Daniel wiped his boots before entering the general store. "Hello stranger, we have not seen you all winter," Mr. Evans greeted jovially.

"It has been a brutal winter. I have not been to town in months," Daniel admitted.

"Your brother was in this morning complaining that the sap is not yet running. The days are well below freezing."

"The Saco is still frozen and I have a fortune in logs stacked on the river bank and a small army of idle men waiting for the spring melt."

"Business has been slow here also," Mr. Evans shook his head.

"Danny, last week you received a letter posted from Biddeford, but it is not from your sister," Mrs. Evans remarked as she went to retrieve the letter.

The letter was addressed to *Mr. Daniel Miller, brother to Rachel Miller, Fryeburg, Maine.*

With apprehension he opened the letter.

March 1, 1850
Biddeford, Maine

Dear Mr. Miller,

It is against your sister's expressed wishes that I write you this letter. I am at my wit's end and feel I can no longer handle this situation. Rachel fell ill a week before Christmas. I take great pride in caring for my girls. At first I was not alarmed for many come down with a fever, cough and chills. Against my advice, she continued to go to work, walking in this frigid weather.

Two weeks after Christmas, she grew weaker as her cough grew stronger and she no longer went to work. At first I believed that was a good thing because with rest, your mother's remedies and my good care she would quickly recover.

Three weeks later I became concerned that this may be more serious than the grippe and she would get the other girls sick. Therefore I isolated her in my own bedroom and dozed in my rocking chair at night. Her lack of working did not create a financial hardship for she had dutifully saved her money. As long as she paid her rent, I was content to have her with me.

Last month the mill fired her for lack of service. Two weeks ago I was told that the boarding house is for employees only and Rachel must leave. The next day a new girl arrived to take Rachel's place.

With assistance from my church, we packed her trunk and belongings in a borrowed wagon and I settled her in at the Cooper's Inn. I cannot adequately care her for I have responsibilities at the boarding house.

This morning I went to visit and found her weak and delirious. The thought of your poor sister dying alone when she has a loving family somewhat nearby breaks my heart.

Please come for your sister as soon as the weather allows.
Yours very truly,
Mrs. Marion Libby

Turning pale, Daniel ran out the door, jumped onto his wagon and headed to Riverview Farm.

Hannah sighed in boredom as Benjamin dozed in his chair, Joshua and Abigail worked in the office and Darian spent his days in school. It had been five months since she and Grace had strolled down Main Street. She immediately realized something was seriously wrong when she watched Daniel pass the house at break neck speed and head to the farm. Politely rapping at the office door, she called, "Quickly run to the farm! I fear something terrible has happened to Emily."

"Mama!" Daniel shouted as he raced into the kitchen. "Rachel is dying!" Tears freely flowed down his cheeks as he handed Kate the letter.

"Get your father," Kate commanded. "Grace, get all the clean linens and blankets in the house." She expertly grabbed her teas, tinctures and poultices. Jacob and Eli ran in from the barn.

"Elijah, ready the wagon and hitch all four of the horses. I shall not be getting stuck in the mud today. I must pack." Jacob wordlessly read the letter.

Joshua and Abigail arrived. "Jacob, Mother is concerned. Is Emily unwell?" she asked.

"Thankfully Emily is fine. It is our Rachel who is dangerously ill," Jacob's voice trembled. "Kate and I will be leaving for Biddeford shortly."

"What can we do?" his sister asked.

"You may pray," he quietly replied. "Abigail, perhaps Isaac could stay with you during our absence. I do not wish to burden Aunt Grace and Sadie with the responsibility of watching him." He was also concerned about leaving an elderly and a deaf woman alone in the house.

"Papa, I can spend the nights here," Eli offered. "Julia will see to it that meals are made and the housework is done."

The wagon was soon loaded. Abigail hugged her brother tightly and Joshua slipped three double eagles into his hand. "There will be expenses," he whispered.

Jacob helped his wife into the wagon, headed down the lane and silently prayed, "Lord please give me the strength to face what I may find in Biddeford."

The weary travelers arrived long after nightfall. As Jacob helped his wife down from the wagon and headed for the door, Kate reminded, "Jacob, my supplies are in the wagon."

"Let us first see what circumstances will greet us," he replied sadly.

"I am sorry but we have no vacancies," the clerk apologized.

"We are here for our daughter. Where may we find her?" Kate demanded.

"Mr. and Mrs. Miller, you have come at last," he said with relief. "We have moved her to the third floor where she was least likely to be disturbed." He led them by lamp light up the narrow stairs to the back bedroom.

"Rachel?" Kate called into the cold darkness. "No fire in the fireplace? No lamp? You keep my daughter in the attic like one of my smoked hams?" Her voice was rising. "Get some wood and a fire going!" she demanded. "I need several kettles of boiling water. Please get someone to help my husband bring up our things." She sat at the edge of the bed, "Rachel, Mama and Papa are here. We will take you home as soon as you are up to it," she stroked her daughter's tangled, curly hair.

It was nearly dawn, when the blaze in the fireplace heated the room, the clean linens and blankets were warmed by the fire and the floors were swept. The hapless clerk had made countless trips up and down the stairs, lugging trunks, carrying two small tables, two wooden chairs, a pitcher, wash basin and a clean chamber pot.

As the early sunlight entered through one curtain less window, Kate was better able to assess the situation. "The room is large enough for all of us. A mattress on the floor in the corner will suffice for now."

"I will get us some breakfast," Jacob volunteered wearily. He silently sat in the corner of the dining room eating fried eggs, potatoes and ham. "I would like to bring up two more breakfasts to my wife and daughter, order three dinners and suppers for the next three days. Also we request another bed to be set up later this morning, please." He handed the clerk a double eagle.

"Yes, sir! Very good, Sir"

Kate was coaxing Rachel to take a sip of yarrow tea to break her fever as Jacob arrived with breakfast. Kate ate hungrily while Jacob sat by Rachel's bedside.

"Kate, you need to get some rest. I will care for her and I will wake you if I need you." Jacob never felt as alone in his life as he watched his wife and daughter sleep. He was accustomed to living in a house filled with people. He thought about the daughter he lost twenty-nine years ago. Rachel's twin had lived barely an hour. How did his brother-in-law survive the loss of his first wife and children? How can Darian cope with the loss of his entire family?

He prayed. He did not bargain with God. He merely asked for the faith to face what lay ahead.

"Mama?" Rachel whispered.

"Mama is here. Kate!" he called. His wife startled from a sound sleep, blinked, stared around the room and then raced to her daughter's side.

"Mama, I am thirsty. Do I have to go to school today?" she mumbled.

"No, dear, you do not have to go anywhere today. Have some more tea." Jacob helped Rachel sit up and she took a few swallows. He patted her forehead with a cool wet towel. She began to cough violently.

"Jacob, please reheat the water to a boil and put a teaspoon of dried mullein leaves in the tea ball. We need to clear these lungs."

"Is it pneumonia?" he whispered.

The door quietly opened and a stooped, elderly man holding a brown leather valise entered. He frowned at the sight of Jacob and Kate.

"Madam, what are you doing?" he demanded.

"I am taking care of my daughter and when she is strong enough I am taking her home. Sir, what are you doing?"

"I am treating my patient. She is dying of consumption."

"Jacob, is the mullein tea ready? She is not dying of consumption. My daughter is suffering from pneumonia and a lack of responsible care," she accused.

"Madam, a cup of tea and old wives tales will not cure your daughter."

"Yarrow tea will break her fever and the mullein tea will clear the congestion in her lungs. She needs plenty of liquids, wholesome food, fresh air and rest. I have treated people sicker than this. I will have her home by next week where she can recover in the comfort of her home and family."

"Madam, your daughter is dying."

"She was dying from neglect. Sir, you may keep your lances and leeches to yourself."

"I insist that I see my patient!"

"I insist that you leave immediately!" Kate countered.

"Sir, what do I owe you for this visit?" Jacob inquired.

"I charge twenty cents for a house call."

"Here is a half dollar–twenty cents for your services and thirty cents to never return. Good day, sir." Jacob held open the door. "My family wishes not to be disturbed."

Kate smiled at her husband in gratitude.

For the next two days Jacob and Kate took turns nursing Rachel. By the third day her fever broke but her wracking cough continued. Jacob scribbled a quick note home to update the family.

On the fifth day, Rachel was sitting up, and taking sips of broth between coughing spasms. They barely heard the rapping on the door. "I asked him not to return," Jacob muttered as he crossed the room to answer the door.

"Isaac!" Jacob exclaimed.

"Mama, you forgot the mustard plaster. I remembered the story of how you treated Danny when he was a baby and had the whooping cough, so I brought the mustard plaster."

"How did you get here?" Jacob asked.

"Sir, I had a delivery to make in Portland," Peter Evans timidly stepped into the room. "I hoped you would forgive my boldness in coming uninvited. The family, indeed half the town, was growing anxious awaiting word. I have a bundle of letters for you and Isaac needed a ride to deliver the mustard plaster."

"I brought a new book, *Moby Dick*. I can read it to Rachel," Isaac offered.

"Peter, how can I ever thank you," Jacob shook his hand. "You two must be hungry after your journey. Let me buy you dinner downstairs while Mrs. Miller applies the plaster," he offered.

"The food is not that good," Isaac warned.

"Thank you, sir. I will have a quick meal before I head back home," Peter explained. "I have a wagon filled with merchandise to return to Fryeburg. Please tell Rachel that I have been thinking of her."

Rachel had no less than thirty-two letters of encouragement, prayers and well wishes. As Kate read each one aloud, she could see Rachel's determination to get well. "We will get you home sometime next week. When you have recovered your strength, you may return to Biddeford if that is your wish or perhaps teach a semester at the Academy," Kate smiled.

"My wish is to go to sleep."

During the next four days, Isaac held the family spell bound as he read from *Moby Dick*. Rachel was able to walk across the room with assistance from her brother.

"You need to eat," Kate scolded.

"I need to go home and eat your cooking," Rachel countered. Kate looked to her husband.

"We will leave first thing tomorrow morning, weather permitting," Jacob promised.

"I will read aloud all the way home," Isaac volunteered.

"No more *Moby Dick*, please!" Rachel pleaded. "I even dream about whales."

"Welcome home," Julia greeted. Kate surveyed the household with a discerning eye. The kitchen was immaculate. Eli had set up a small bed and table in the front parlor for Rachel to rest during the day. "Eli and the children are at the sugar house. Danny has been working nonstop since the ice went out last week. Darian is staying with Danny and Emily to work during the busy season. Aunt Grace is visiting Nana. The house will be peaceful so you may rest," she smiled. "Are you hungry? I can heat up some stew."

"Julia, how can I thank you?" Kate asked wearily.

"Where is Sadie?" Jacob asked.

"She is finishing a painting at the sugar house."

After the four of them had eaten, they exhaustedly fell into their beds.

Despite his protests, Isaac left for school the next day. Kate helped Rachel get settled in the bed downstairs.

Sadie entered the front parlor carrying a book. "I am reading a new book. I thought you might enjoy me reading it aloud to you."

"Not *Moby Dick*," Rachel groaned.

"No. It is called *The Scarlet Letter* by Nathaniel Hawthorn. "Please do not tell your grandmother, for she will be mortified."

"What about your painting?" Rachel asked.

"It is finally finished," Sadie smiled. "I need to take a break before I begin another. Shall we begin?"

At midmorning Grace appeared with a tray of teacups and a plate of biscuits as Kate followed carrying the teapot.

"I missed this while I was away," Rachel pointed to the tea and biscuits. "You could not stop work during the morning to take a break. The machines were so noisy no one can hear you speak."

"I missed having you in the kitchen to talk with," Kate agreed.

Joshua stopped the carriage by the front door and helped Benjamin and Hannah down. Rachel slid *The Scarlet Letter* under her pillow.

"We will not stay long. We know you need your rest," Hannah assured as she entered the room holding her husband's arm.

"A year and a half is much too long to go without seeing my favorite granddaughter," Benjamin greeted. "I had to come see you for myself."

Rachel made a slow but steady recovery. Gradually she took on some of her previous household duties. Although she tired easily, she took brief rests and returned to the project at hand. One sunny June morning she announced, "I intend to take a walk to visit Grandpa and Nana."

Hannah was thrilled when Rachel appeared at the back door. "This is certainly the answer to my prayers! You are looking well! Your grandfather is napping in his chair. Do you feel up to taking a walk to the general store to post these letters?"

Rachel could feel her strength giving out as she held the letters in one hand and opened the door to the store with the other. Her eyes struggled to adjust to the dim light. The pungent aromas overwhelmed her and the loud voices grew dimmer. She dropped the letters on the floor.

"Miss Miller?" Peter Evans put his arm around her waist and guided her to a nearby chair.

Mrs. Evans came bustling over. "Peter, please take Rachel upstairs where it is quiet and get her something to drink," she suggested. "Your father needs me in the store."

"What is this?" Rachel asked after taking her first gulp of the unfamiliar beverage.

"It is called lemonade. We squeeze the juice from lemons, add sugar and water. I thought you would prefer this over rum," he joked.

"You thought correctly. May I have another cup?"

He refilled. "Mother thinks you have over exerted yourself and suggests that you rest and have plenty to drink."

"I think she may be right."

"When do you think you will be returning to work?" he tried to appear nonchalant.

"I am not certain that I shall."

"You have earned enough money to go to school?"

"I have not thought what I shall do next. May I ask you a personal question?"

"I have no secrets," he replied. The two of them had known each other all their lives. Although they attended school together, it was from her dealings at the store where she came to know this quiet and serious young man.

"Were you disappointed that you did not attend Bowdoin College?" Fifteen years ago Peter's older brother drowned in the Saco River. As the oldest son Michael was to inherit the store. Mr. Evans was going to finance Peter's education. However, after his brother's death, Peter stayed home to work in the family business.

"I had planned on becoming a minister and going out west to Wisconsin to start a church and a school. When my parents were devastated by Michael's death, I knew I could not leave for school that September. I told them that I would stay home for a year to help them and then I would leave to pursue my studies.

I discovered that I enjoy working in the store. I enjoy meeting the customers but I like the challenge of finding new merchandise at the best prices in Boston and Portland to sell back here. It is much more than buying and selling items. Some of these older people are lonely and need a place to meet people. When Widow Dresser was left penniless, I found a store in Boston that would sell her braided rugs for a very good price. I also accepted old woolen rags or clothes as credit on people's accounts and then turned over the fabrics to Mrs. Dresser. She has free wool, people have credit to buy merchandise and I make a modest fee for selling her rugs in Boston."

"Peter, that was brilliant. I had no idea."

"I decided that I could serve the Lord here as well as on the frontier. I must admit that my life has not gone as I had planned. My father always says you have to grow where you are planted."

"That sounds like wise advice."

That Sunday morning Rachel donned her green dress with the white flowers. "I feel well enough to attend church. I do not wish to miss the dedication of the new church building," she declared.

"You and I will sit in the back row by the door. If you feel a coughing spell coming on, I will take you home," Kate fretted.

Rachel opened her mouth to protest but a knowing glance from her father stopped her.

"Aunt Grace, you look lovely this morning," Jacob complimented.

"I must tell you I feared I would not live long enough to see this day. I have never seen such slow workers in my life."

"Rome was not built in a day," Jacob reminded.

"Why Darian, look at you all dressed up," Hannah complimented with surprise at breakfast.

"Do you think I would let you miss the dedication of your church?"

"Do you mean you are coming to church with me?"

"Just this once."

The entire town of Fryeburg was headed toward the new white building with the towering spire. "Where were half of these people last week?" Grace huffed. "Even the Unitarians are here!"

"Aunt Grace, we should be thankful that so many of our good neighbors have come to hear the Gospel," Jacob patted her hand.

Darian helped Hannah down from the carriage as Joshua assisted his father-in-law. Abigail took her father's arm and the five of them slowly ascended the wooden steps. Darian thought the white pillars looked more like a Greek temple than a church. There were three doorways to enter and he followed Abigail and Benjamin through the center double doors. He looked around for a basin of holy water. When he found none he simply made the sign of the cross. He was disappointed when he entered the sanctuary. Where were the statues? It looked plain to him with three sections of wooden seats and white walls. He followed Benjamin down the front where the Millers owned the first three rows of the center. No one genuflected before sitting down.

The minister preached in English and not Latin. He remembered Benjamin telling him that men like Tyndale risked their lives to print the Bible in English so everyone could read and understand it for himself. He was relieved that no one served communion for he had not gone to confession for years. Then he remembered Hannah once told him that they took communion once a month. "Protestants are strange," he thought. He did enjoy the singing. He remembered singing with his family back in Ireland before the starving days.

Kate looked on in concern as Rachel muffled her cough. "Mother, I am fine," she whispered. From the back row she had the advantage of observing the entire congregation – the pious, the bored, the young fidgeting in their seats, a few of the elderly nodding off, her extended family sitting together in the front rows. How she had missed them and how she had cherished their letters from home. She was uncertain if she could leave them again. For now she was content to remain in Fryeburg.

XV

The Proprietress

The following evening Mrs. Evans and her son Peter arrived at the front door of Riverview Farm.

"Do come in," Grace invited. "It is a lovely evening for a walk."

Mrs. Evans looked around the front parlor with admiration. "I have come to inquire about Rachel's health."

"Mrs. Evans, how kind of you to stop by," Rachel entered. "I am doing well. I thank you for your concern."

"Would you be interested in working in the store a few hours in the mornings? I have more responsibilities than I can handle."

"What would be my duties?"

"I need someone to help the customers while I get caught up on paperwork. You may work until you feel tired. Then I shall have Peter take you home in the carriage. Perhaps he could pick you up in the mornings as well. There is no need to tire yourself before you begin work."

"I practically grew up in that store! I know where everything is and I know the customers. Peter, what time shall I expect you to pick me up?"

"Seven o'clock?"

Rachel smiled. "I shall see you at seven."

The Proprietress

By nine o'clock the next morning half the village had heard that Rachel Miller was working at the general store and several ladies arrived to learn the details.

"Rachel, you poor dear, I hear that working in those mills is simply dreadful," Mrs. Osgood began.

"It is no more difficult than working on a farm. May I show you some fabric? A new shipment of lace just arrived yesterday and I have not had the opportunity to put it out." Mrs. Osgood bought four yards of lace.

"I understand that many fathers send their daughters to work in the mills to pay off the mortgage on their farms," Mrs. Pike suggested.

"I believe that is true. One young lady in my boarding house came to work for those very reasons. Mrs. Pike, how may I help you today?" she smiled.

Mrs. Pike paid cash for five pounds of coffee which she did not need.

"Is it true what they say about those boarding houses?" Mrs. Bradley whispered.

"What do they say about those boarding houses?" Rachel whispered back. "Our house was meticulous but the food was not as good as at home. The other girls were lovely. Not growing up with sisters, I did appreciate the company of my housemates."

Mrs. Merrill stood nearby eavesdropping. "Mrs. Merrill, please forgive me. Here I am chatting away why you patiently wait for me to wait on you. Did you hear that we just received a shipment of embroidery hoops? My brother, Daniel, says that white ash makes the best hoops. Do you need a new one or were you here to buy more thread?"

By noon sales had increased by 25% from the previous day.

On Saturday afternoon Mr. Evans tentatively approached Rachel. "I fear I cannot pay you as much as the mill did.

Here are two dimes plus a dollar's worth of your own credit at the store."

She tried to conceal her disappointment as she graciously took the coins. However with no expenses for room and board, she could keep all of her money plus buy books, fabric and anything else she wanted from the store.

"May I take you home?" Peter offered.

"I am feeling quite well enough to walk back myself. I may visit my grandparents first. I do not wish to bother you."

"It is no bother! I enjoy taking you home," he replied a little too eagerly.

"Perhaps you may escort me to my grandparents," she smiled. They strolled down Main Street for Peter was in no hurry. "May I ask you another personal question?"

"I have no secrets."

"Why have you not married?" she blurted.

"I am neither handsome, rich nor a farmer. Apparently those are the three most important attributes to Fryeburg women. Why have you not married? It is only fair, you asked me first."

"I refuse to marry a handsome, wealthy farmer!" she joked.

By the end of the summer Rachel was able to work a full day with a couple of breaks to sit and rest. Peter continued to pick her up each morning although she insisted on walking home after work. Her dimes were slowly accumulating and she bought fabric for two new dresses. Grace and Hannah volunteered to sew them for her.

"Rachel, are these fancy dresses really necessary?" her grandmother challenged.

"Hannah, it is good business. When the ladies of Fryeburg see the fabric modeled by an attractive, young woman, they will want to buy it for themselves," Grace explained although she suspected there may be another reason.

It was a brisk September morning when Rachel walked to work with her shawl draped over her shoulders. Peter was away on business in Boston. Mrs. Evans anxiously opened the door. "Do you think you can run the store by yourself? Mr. Evans is feeling poorly and I am on my way to fetch Dr. Barrows."

Rachel swept the floors and tidied up the store before the United States mail arrived. She placed the few envelopes in the mail slots.

"I am sorry, but I do not have the authority to purchase any inventory in Mr. Evans' absence," she explained to one gentleman who wanted to barter some chickens for rum. "Do you wish to make your purchase with cash? Or perhaps you have a credit to your account which I could debit?" she replied sweetly. He angrily muttered under his breath and left the store.

"That was very wise of you, Rachel," Mrs. Hurd complimented.

"I know. Those were not his chickens."

By noon, most of the village had heard the general store was only accepting cash or deducting customer's accounts. No credit would be given until Peter returned or Mr. Evans recovered. Grudgingly, most people parted with their hard earned money.

The next morning a somber Reverend Hurd unlocked the store door for her. "Please come in," he invited wearily. "Mr. Evans died earlier this morning. Mrs. Evans is expecting Peter today or tomorrow and she would like you to keep the store open."

Within the hour the curious and the concerned crowded the store plying Rachel with questions. Some were dismayed that Mrs. Evans would open the store under the circumstances; others were grateful for the opportunity to shop.

It was past closing time when a discouraged Peter with a wagon half filled with merchandise pulled up to the back of the store. He had barely sold his goods at a profitable price while he paid more than he deemed necessary for his purchases.

Rachel discretely slipped out the back door to greet him.

"Was it a busy day? Why are so many people still here?" he asked.

"Peter, your father has not been well this week. Please run upstairs to see your mother. I shall recruit some men to unload the wagon. We can take care of this tomorrow."

Peter's older sister ran to his side and burst into tears. "I thought you would never get home! Whatever shall we do without Father?"

A stricken Peter silently followed his sister upstairs to their apartment.

Evans General Store remained empty while the Congregational Church was full the day of Edward Evans' funeral. The next morning Rachel tentatively approached the closed sign displayed in the door. An exhausted Peter unlocked the door.

"Peter, I was uncertain if the store would be open today but I wish to help you in anyway."

"Your family's kindness since my father's death is greatly appreciated. Please continue the practice of cash only or debit their credit," he handed her the ledger. "Please call me if someone wishes to sell anything. I will be upstairs."

"Try to get some rest," she gently patted his arm.

The store was quiet that day as the farmers and families were busy with their harvests. Rachel kept herself busy sweeping and straightening up.

A disheveled Peter came downstairs just as Rachel was going to close up. "I have been going over the books all day," he shook his head. "I would never ask you this, if it was not an emergency. I know that you saved some money while you were at the mill. Would you consider giving me a loan? I will pay you back with interest in two months. After harvest most of my customers will pay their debts and…"

"Of course. How much do you need?"

"Fifteen hundred dollars."

Rachel gasped. "I could loan you a hundred dollars, but I do not have money like that."

Peter look crushed. "Please forgive me for asking. I fear I am not thinking clearly."

"My grandfather might be willing. I shall speak to him."

The next evening a very uncomfortable Peter sat silently watching Benjamin study three years' of ledgers. Finally Benjamin cleared his throat. "Peter, your father was a kind man but a poor businessman. I cannot possibly loan you any money under these present circumstances."

"Sir, thank you for your time," Peter stood up.

"Please be seated, son," Benjamin spoke kindly. "I understand you are not responsible for this current fiscal crisis. If you are willing to take some advice, you may find yourself in improved circumstances and in need of less money. I may consider a loan under those circumstances."

"Yes, sir. What do you suggest?"

"First, you cannot extend unlimited credit to everyone for any purchase. I understand that many of our neighbors have seasonal incomes and may be in temporary need of credit. Lending them credit is good business. However, look at your day books. Some people are trustworthy. Others," he pointed to a few names, "are not. These people must be denied any future credit until their bills are paid. Some items such as farm implements or tools are needed to earn their livings. They could be sold on credit. People can live without luxuries such as rum, tobacco, lace, books; they should be willing to pay cash for these.

I see your father had generously extended credit to two families who are truly in need. He should be commended. I will pay these debts plus interest tonight. Tomorrow I will discuss these families' plights with the church elders. There may be members of the congregation who are willing to share from their abundance." Benjamin opened the top drawer, pulled out a leather pouch and handed him a gold double eagle. "Please keep me apprised of your progress. Do not be discouraged for you are a good son and a hard working young man. I am confident this is merely a temporary setback."

"Thank you, sir."

Rachel spent the next day writing up invoices accompanied by a carefully worded letter of explanation of the new credit policy and placed them in people's mailboxes. Reactions were swift and mixed.

"I will take my business elsewhere," Mrs. Page declared.

"Where will you shop? This is the only store in Fryeburg," level headed Mrs. Osgood pointed out.

"I pay my bills and I expect others to do so as well," Mr. Weston stated indignantly.

"I would sure hate to see a few irresponsible people put Peter Evans out of business!" another complained.

Some people said nothing and sheepishly deposited nickels and dimes toward their debts.

Daniel and Emily paid cash for fifty yards of simple but sturdy fabrics plus a sundry of notions. "I plan to get an early start on my sewing this winter," she pleasantly explained. Peter smiled his gratitude.

Early one morning Widow Merrill approached the counter and handed Rachel a half penny. "Why Mrs. Merrill you do not owe us any money. Your debt has been paid in full."

"There must be some mistake," she stammered.

Peter walked over and examined the ledger. "You are correct. It appears that you have a credit. Do you need anything today? I am about to make a delivery in East Fryeburg and I would be happy to drop off any items at your home on my way."

On a cold, December evening a more relaxed Peter Evans sat with Benjamin in the front parlor with Rachel, Joshua, Abigail and Hannah. "Sir, I thank you for your advice. We have taken in over seven hundred dollars and I am in need of only $750.00.

"I am pleased to hear that. However I decided against the loan. If I loaned you any money at my age I would be long gone before it was repaid."

"I understand, sir. I do thank you for your advice."

"However, if you are looking for some investors, I may have found some business partners."

"I am willing to invest $250.00 and free legal services for a small percentage of the business," Joshua offered.

"Thank you, Mr. Pierce. I could benefit from your experience and advice."

"Grandpa has given me my inheritance. I have decided against attending Mt. Holyoke and becoming a teacher. During my absence my mother found other family members to assist her with her responsibilities. I would like to invest an additional $500.00, become your business partner and live here to help my aunt and my grandparents."

"My mother has decided to move to Brownfield to live with my sister. I was afraid I would have to run this business alone. It would be wonderful to have partners."

"Then I will write up the contracts," Joshua agreed.

Rachel stopped and admired the newly painted sign which read *Evans' and Miller's General Store* as she took out her key and unlocked the front door. Peter entered from the back room and greeted her with a smile.

"I would like to discuss some changes I would like to make," she began.

"I am sure you do," he laughed.

"I think we should discontinue selling rum and whiskey."

"That would make the ladies of the Maine Temperance Society happy. May I remind you this store makes a handsome profit from these items?"

"That is not true. I have been studying the ledgers. You may sell a lot of rum, but it is often on credit and it takes a while to get paid, if we get paid in full at all. Certain customers barely pay their tabs before buying more. You have money tied up for months."

"I will study the matter. Perhaps I will locate the rum in a less visible spot and prominently display our local cider."

Also we should no longer sell white sugar and coffee because sugar cane and coffee beans are picked by slaves."

"Although I have the highest respect for your family's ideals, there are many in Fryeburg who disagree. I dare say there are several people who believe if the Union should ever dissolve, it will be the fault of the fanatical abolitionists."

"Shall I remain silent in the face of evil because of a neighbor's discomfort?" she challenged.

"If you wish people to respect your views, you must show respect for theirs," he countered.

"Even if they are wrong?"

"Some people may call you self-righteous. Who are you to judge others? I will agree to sell down on the white sugar. It is too expensive for most of our customers and maple sugar is widely available at a much lower price. I will not give up on coffee. Customers should shop according to their consciences and not be scolded by the shopkeeper. Do you plan to discontinue selling cotton fabric? Cotton is picked by slaves," he challenged.

"I have given that some thought."

"I am sure you have."

"I would like to invite some local ladies to sell their homespun linen and wool on consignment. They may earn some extra money without any financial risk to us. This will also give our customers the opportunity to shop according to their consciences.

I would also like to expand our literary selection."

"Where do we have room for this?"

"With a little rearranging and elimination of excess inventory, I believe I can make room."

"People will not be able to find things if you begin shuffling merchandise around."

"Or people may spy old merchandise in new locations. Also we should ban the chewing of tobacco in the store. It is a disgusting habit and the ladies do not like it.

Also those horse blankets have not sold in five years. We should mark down the price. We could use the space for more marketable merchandise. We do not need five barrels of flour taking up floor space. Let us keep two out and put the other three barrels in the back room. That will create more space. I asked Isaac and Darian to stop by after school to help with the rearranging."

"Are we going to talk all day or shall I open the store?" a flustered Peter asked.

Rachel took out a long list from her apron pocket, "We can continue talking while the store is open.

Good morning Mr. Frye," she greeted Julia's father. "The farmer's almanac predicts it will be a very cold winter. We are selling horse blankets at half price and we still have a few left."

Peter looked on in disbelief as she sold two of them. Rachel smiled for she enjoyed being a proprietress.

XVI

Just a Farmer

Elijah James Miller whistled as he and his three children walked across Weston's Bridge on a glorious January morning. The thermometer on the side of his house had read 33 degrees and the snow sparkled in the sunlight. Everyone and everything he loved was within walking distance.

Thirteen- year old Becky would make a fine farmer's wife one day. Demonstrating great culinary skills she was an asset to her mother and grandmother. In contrast eleven- year old Victoria enjoyed helping her mother sew clothes for the family. Seven- year old Davy was devoted to caring for the livestock.

He stopped for a second to study the scene before him. The farmhouse and fields were enveloped in forty shades of white against an azure sky. The bright red barn and his father's brown coat contrasted against the snow. Eli could not understand how his sister would choose to leave this idyllic life to work in a mill or a store. He could not forgive Thaddeus for abandoning the family; his parents had heard nothing from him in almost two years.

Isaac ran out the side door carrying his books and lunch pail to join his nieces and nephew in their walk to school. Their voices and laughter carried across the frozen fields.

"Good morning," his father greeted. "I need you to climb to the hayloft and throw down some hay." Eli understood that his father's achy knees prevented him from climbing the ladder.

After completing that task Eli offered, "I thought I would shovel the front steps and a path to the road. If there was ever a fire I fear Aunt Grace could never make it from the front parlor to the side door," he worried.

Jacob nodded with appreciation.

"Isaac is old enough to shovel," Eli reminded his father.

"That is true enough," Jacob agreed. "However I prefer that he spends his free time helping his mother with the apothecary. He knows how to make all the tinctures, oils and salves and the market prices for each. There are left over biscuits and butter waiting for you when you are finished," he invited.

Ten minutes later, Eli surprised Grace when he entered through the front door. "Aunt Grace, how is your book coming along?"

She looked up and placed her quill in the ink well. "I am up to the year 1806 when they built the new Fryeburg Academy at its present location."

"Do you mean there was an old Fryeburg Academy somewhere else?" he asked puzzle.

"Does this generation know nothing about their town? It was at the corner of Main Street and River Street, right across the street from your grandparents' home."

"I will be the first one to read your book when you are finished," he promised. "Where is Sadie?"

"She is upstairs in Rachel's old room. She has turned that into her studio."

Eli ran up the front stairs taking two steps at a time. He knocked on the opened door, but she did not hear. He walked to her side studying the painting of the entire Miller family husking corn in the barn.

"I call this the *Husking Bee*," she quietly explained.

Eli knelt beside her and spoke slowly and clearly. "You must come outside with me and see how beautiful the farm looks in the snow. You must paint this. No one can create shades of white like you can."

Sadie laughed out loud, "Eli you should have been an artist! You have an eye for beauty."

Eli shook his head, "You say I should have been an artist, Grandpa says I should have been a lawyer."

"No your grandfather says you should have been the President of the United States," she corrected.

"Nana, says I should have been a preacher. But I am happy to be just a farmer." Eli held Sadie's arm as they walked down to the covered bridge.

"It is breathtaking!" she agreed. "I can envision my father hitching his horses to his sleigh."

"I can help you set up the easel and paints right here under cover," he offered. Sadie's smile was his reward.

An hour later he entered the kitchen where he found his parents and Aunt Grace eating buttered biscuits. "That was very kind of you, Elijah," Grace commended.

"The only thing I appreciate about winter is I have time to sit down," Eli stated as he buttered two biscuits and took a sip of cider.

"Please do not get too comfortable, I need you to go to the general store and buy some hinges," Jacob said as he picked up another biscuit.

"Do you really need hinges or do you want me to check up on Rachel?" Eli questioned.

"Both."

"Perhaps I will visit Nana and Grandpa and see if they need anything."

"Your grandfather will enjoy that. I am not sure how many winters he has left," Grace sighed.

Eli whistled as he strolled up the lane and knocked on the back door of his grandparents' house. Hannah greeted him with a big smile. "What a surprise! Come in! It has been a long winter and it is good to see a familiar face."

"How are you Nana?" he gave her a big hug before hanging up his coat. "Darian did a good job shoveling the steps and walkway. Let me throw a little more wood in the stove."

"We are well. Darian does the chores, Rachel does the cooking, Joshua runs the office and Abigail keeps us company. Your grandfather will be so pleased to see you."

"Good morning, Grandpa," Eli greeted Benjamin who was reading *The House of the Seven Gables* by Nathaniel Hawthorne.

"The only good thing about winter is you have time to visit your old grandpa. I think I found a new book for our book discussion."

"Please not another book! I just finished reading *Moby Dick*."

"What did you think?"

"I think I am happy to be a farmer and I will never set foot on a boat. What do you think of our new President Millard Fillmore?"

Benjamin shook his head, "He will never amount to anything. The only reason he is president is because Zachary Taylor died. He will never win an election on his own. He is a spineless northerner who will not stand up to the South. He has been President for only six months and he supported the Compromise of 1850 and enforced the Fugitive Slave Act.[1] He is a disgrace to the Whig Party."

"Some might say he is trying to hold the country together by compromise," Eli suggested.

"Christians should never compromise with evil, no matter the cost. I want you to always remember that."

"Yes, sir. I am on my way to the general store, do you need anything?" Eli was quick to change the subject for he disliked seeing his grandfather agitated.

"I have some letters to mail. Perhaps you can check to see if your aunt has any mail as well. You have always been a good boy, Eli," he patted his grandson's arm.

"Even though I am just a farmer and not the President?" he teased.

"You would be a better president than Millard Fillmore!"

Eli entered the crowded store where he overhead a couple of old men sitting by the woodstove grumbling they could not chew tobacco. "This is what happens when petticoats take over a business."

"You could go home and chew tobacco," Eli pointed out good naturedly. He eyed his sister speaking with an irate costumer.

"Miss Miller, I clearly stated when I bought these cedar shingles from Mr. Evans yesterday that I wanted them to be delivered today!"

"I am sorry, sir but Mr. Evans is in Portland and will not be back until late tomorrow."

"Where do they need to be delivered?" Eli interrupted.

"In Brownfield, on Hayley Town Road."

"Rachel, please mail these letters, I will go back to the farm to get the sleigh. Sir, you will have your shingles by midafternoon."

Eli was slightly out of breath as he hurried back to the farm.

"How is your grandfather?" Kate asked as he entered the warm kitchen.

"He is upset with Millard Fillmore."

"Do you have the hinges?" Jacob asked.

"No, I forgot. Pa, would you like to take a ride to Brownfield with me? Rachel needs me to deliver some shingles."

Father and son returned to the store, loaded the shingles onto the sleigh and headed to Brownfield.

"It seems like nobody is content to stay in Fryeburg anymore. Young men are off to find work in the cities or to prospect for gold in California or to settle out west," Jacob lamented. "No one wants to be a farmer these days. I am grateful that you will take over the farm someday."

"The problem is people do not recognize the skill and knowledge it takes to farm. There are new ideas and improvements every day, but we farmers stick to ourselves. We should get together to share ideas and help each other out. I hear there are towns that have fairs which award prizes for the best livestock or corn. Maybe Fryeburg could have a fair. We could discuss it with Mr. Weston."

It was a cold spring day on March 27, 1851 when several businessmen from the towns of Hiram, Brownfield and Fryeburg met at Sam Stickney's Inn in Brownfield to discuss forming an agricultural society.[2] Eli stifled a yawn for he had been up late every night for the past three weeks cooking down sap into sugar. The seasonal variety of chores is what endeared him to farming. He was an outdoors man of action who quickly grew bored sitting indoors listening to tedious details. He thanked the Good Lord that he did not listen to his grandfather and become a lawyer; he loved being just a farmer.

"To form the West Oxford Agricultural Society we must elect officers and then apply to the Maine State Legislature for an Act of Incorporation," Mr. Osgood explained.

"Next we must draw up a constitution,"[3] Mr. Souther continued.

Now Eli was well versed with the American Constitution and the Maine State Constitution, thanks to his grandfather. But farmers need a constitution to farm? "The object of the Society should be in the improvement of agriculture and horticulture," Eli contributed.

"Excellent! Mr. Miller, would you care to join Mr. Souther and me to draft a constitution?" Mr. Osgood invited.

"Well what I had in mind was to plan the events and to invite one to two hundred people in the outlying towns to join the society," Eli explained.

"What other towns would you include?" Peleg Wadsworth, the newly elected president of the Society asked.

"I was thinking we should include the good citizens of Porter, Denmark, Lovell, Sweden, Stow, Waterford and Stoneham in addition to Fryeburg, Hiram and Brownfield."[4]

"That's an excellent suggestion! Shall we make a motion?" asked attorney and vice-president of the Society, David Hastings.

"We can hold our first fair in Hiram," President Wadsworth and Hiram resident invited.

"I thought we could award prizes for best acre of corn, best seed corn, best seed wheat, apples, dairy, cloth, leather and harnesses, agricultural tools, cows, oxen and fowls," Eli was growing excited at the potential of this fair.

The topic of discussion at Evans' & Miller's General Store was the new agricultural fair. People were plying Eli with questions when he entered the store with the intent to mail a letter for his grandfather.

"How do we join?" Fryeburg farmers asked.

"Why is there nothing for the ladies?" Rachel questioned her brother. "You should award prizes for the best apple pie or embroidery or quilt."

"Why is it just for farmers and not for woodsmen?' his brother Daniel asked. "We could have contests in wood chopping, log rolling, buck sawing and tree felling,"[5] he suggested.

"Danny, it is an agricultural fair and not a sawyer's fair," Eli impatiently explained.

"Why is it in Hiram? Why not hold it in Fryeburg?" Peter asked for he foresaw increased business having hundreds of new people visiting town."

"It will be in Fryeburg in '52 and Lovell in '53. The surrounding towns will take a turn hosting the fair," Eli explained.

"Son, take my advice. You need a permanent site and you need to locate it in Fryeburg," Mr. Weston explained.

"Yes, sir. I will see what I can do in the future. Excuse me; I must get back to the sugar bush for the sap is still running." Eli turned to leave.

"Are you going to mail Grandpa's letter?" Rachel reminded her brother.

He handed it over. What did he get himself into? He was no organizer, he was just a farmer.

XVII

The Journey from California

The stage coach stopped in front of the Oxford House and a well- dressed young man stepped down, grabbed two large leather satchels and strolled toward the large white house on the corner. "Nothing ever changes in Fryeburg," he mused as he headed toward the back door.

Joshua saw him first through his office window. Should he feel gratitude that his son was alive or anger for not maintaining contact with the family? He put down his quill, quietly left the office and entered the front parlor where Benjamin was dozing, Hannah and Abigail were sewing.

"Darian is growing like a weed," Abigail explained. "I need to take down the hems on all his trousers. What is wrong?"

"He is here," Joshua quietly stated as not to wake his father-in-law.

"Thaddeus is home!" she excitedly declared as she ran to the kitchen door.

"Thaddeus is home!" Darian and Isaac came running down the stairs.

Benjamin's eyes flew open. "Thaddeus is home, dear," Hannah calmly informed him.

"So I have heard."

"I have been worried sick about you!" Abigail greeted her son at the door as she embraced him.

The Journey from California

"You should have written," Joshua admonished.

"I have been busy," he shrugged.

"The important thing is he is home safe and sound," Abigail sighed with relief.

"The Prodigal Son has returned," Thaddeus laughed.

"Welcome home," Hannah smiled warmly and opened her arms.

"Nana, you have not changed a bit. You are looking well," he awkwardly hugged his grandmother. "And who is this young man?" he pointed to a grinning Darian. "You must have grown six inches! Where is Grandpa?" he worriedly looked around.

"Shall we join him in the front parlor?" Hannah invited as the family followed her.

"Grandpa, I came as soon as I received everyone's letters when I arrived back in New York," Thaddeus explained. "You must understand I cannot always be contacted when I am at work, nor should you expect to hear from me.

When I left for California two years, I did not expect that I would be gone this long. I originally planned to take a clipper ship for the seventeen thousand mile trip between New York and San Francisco around Cape Horn. But once I was on board I did not think I could face over a hundred days at sea.[1]

Instead I opted to take a steamship to Central America and cross overland by way of the Isthmus of Panama and take the first ship I could on the Pacific side to San Francisco. Once in Panama we traveled fifty miles by dugout canoe up the Chagres River through jungles. Next we rented donkeys and traveled through more jungles and mountains. The heat, humidity and mosquitoes were a nightmare. People were getting sick with malaria, yellow fever and typhoid.[2] When I contracted yellow fever, my group continued without me. After a three week convalescence I continued my trek to Panama City on the Pacific Coast. When I arrived I discovered that my traveling companions had departed without me on the steamer

California. I had no choice but to wait for the ship to return and pick up more passengers. The city was overwhelmed with potential gold prospectors and rooms cost up to $10.00 per day. It was weeks before another ship was available. When I finally booked passage on a ship for $400.00 and landed in San Francisco, I still had to travel inland to Sutter's Mill.[3] By the time I reached my final destination, I was depleted of funds."

"How could you afford your trip home?" Abigail asked.

"There was plenty of gold to be had," he replied vaguely.

"You went mining for gold?" Isaac asked.

"Mining is hard work. If you must know I won it in poker games," he winked at his cousin.

"Thaddeus!" his mother gasped.

"Do not blame me if those fools were willing to drink away and gamble their hard earned gold. If they were going to lose it to someone, it might as well be me," he laughed. "Or they would have just spent it on the women."

"Were there lady prospectors too?" Isaac asked innocently.

"Perhaps you two boys could run up to the farm and let the family know that Thaddeus has arrived," Hannah suggested.

"Would you like to get settled in your room before supper?" Abigail asked failing in her attempts to hide her fluster.

"First we have business to discuss," Benjamin slowly stood up and grabbed his cane. Joshua and Thaddeus followed him into the office.

"Did you receive my letter?" Benjamin asked.

"I received two years' worth of letters when I arrived back in New York. That is why I returned home."

"I am offering you a partnership in this law firm. Your father cannot carry on alone for much longer. In my will I am leaving the house to your parents with the stipulation that if you are a law partner the house will in turn be left to you and your heirs," Benjamin offered.

"You have had several years of travel but now it is time for you to settle down. Your family needs you here," Joshua continued.

"I have no intentions of becoming a small town lawyer for I am returning to Europe. I am writing a book on the greed and lawlessness of capitalism as demonstrated at the California Gold Rush. Also I will research Marx and Engels and the inroads of socialism in Europe."

"How will you live?"

"Gold speaks the universal language."

"Are you telling me that traveling around with Karl Marx and Friedrich Engels takes precedence over your responsibilities to your family?" Joshua challenged.

"There is a whole big world outside of Fryeburg filled with new and exciting ideas," Thaddeus countered." I have witnessed the evil of capitalism first hand. I have seen what gold fever can do to a man. I have watched the oppressed masses barely survive on starvation wages and cruel working conditions in the textile mills in England. I have seen starving children in Ireland and revolutions in Europe. Capitalism will not, it must not, survive."

"You are an impressionable young man lacking in discernment. A new and exciting idea does not mean it is a good one," Benjamin explained to his grandson. "I fear your education has surpassed your wisdom. I think after a few years at home you will be better grounded to objectively evaluate different theories."

Thaddeus bit his tongue for he knew he was no match to debate his grandfather.

"After I read your article on Marx, I did some research of my own. You are not the only one with contacts in Europe. Your Mr. Marx never did a day's work of manual labor in his life. Born to a wealthy German family, he attended the University of Bonn and the University of Berlin before he married an educated baroness of the Prussian ruling class. I hardly call that the childhood of a proletariat. He spent most of his time writing and getting exiled from Germany before moving to France. When the French government expelled him he moved to Brussels and from there to England where he now resides.[4]

How does he support himself and his family? His partner Friedrich Engels financially supports him. Where does Mr. Engels get that kind of money? Mr. Engels was born into a family of wealthy cotton merchants in Manchester, England. Capitalism is financing their Communist Revolution,"[5] Joshua explained

Thaddeus was speechless. "Does this surprise you? Perhaps you need to better research your subject. Let us set aside these facts for one moment and study his theories.

His first mistake is he makes a universal generalization from a simple single example. The cotton industry represents capitalism and he assumes that all other industries would follow. He assumes that all factory workers who he labels the proletariat want a revolution. Has he ever worked in a mill? Does he actually know any factory workers? If he did, he would know that workers do not want revolution, they want higher wages and better working conditions.[6] All you had to do was ask your cousin Rachel.

Where have the European revolutions occurred?"

"In Italy and Hungary."

"Were there revolutions in England or Belgium?"

"No sir."

"Yet England and Belgium are the two most highly industrialized nations in Europe. The revolutions occurred in the backward countries not the industrialized ones. It was the lack of capitalism not capitalism which fed the 1848 revolutions. The fundamental cause was as the population increased in the rural areas, people crowded into the cities where there were too few jobs to employ them.[7]

His second mistake was he assumes that revolution is the only way to enact political change. Universal suffrage is a powerful weapon against tyranny. In France Napoleon III was overthrown, not for a classless society but for a Republic.

His third mistake is he assumes that the conflict exists only between the classes and not within the classes.[8] He assumes that the workers of the world will unite. Look at Europe. Nationalism is a stronger force than economics. The Italian states unified into one nation; the German states unified into their own nation; Hungary wants to separate from the Austrian Hungarian Empire to become its own nation. These people wish to unite on the basis of a common language and culture and not divide internationally along class lines.[9]

There is enough evil to fight in this country; it is called slavery. Use your God-given talents, your intellect, your writing to combat slavery. Get involved in politics. Study the Constitution not Marxism."

"I am sorry that I have failed to live up to your expectations of me. I am sorry but I will be returning to Europe."

"You are throwing your life away!" Joshua pounded his fist on the table in a rare display of anger.

"Since when did we Millers agree on politics?" Benjamin intervened. "You should have witnessed the arguments my brother Micah and I had over Federalism and Shays Rebellion! You will always be my grandson. This is America. A man has a right to his political decisions."

"Thank you Grandpa."

"Do I understand that inheritance is an anathema to Socialists?"

"Yes, sir. That is one of the tenants of Marxism."

"Let me illustrate my respect for your beliefs. I would never insult you by leaving this property to you. I will rewrite my will and leave it to Isaac. This works out perfectly – Elijah inherits the farm, Daniel inherits the saw mill and Rachel has inherited some cash which she wisely invested. Isaac will inherit this property after your parents are gone and you will live the life of a European socialist. Of course your bedroom will always be available when you visit. You are always welcome here."

All his life Thaddeus had heard his grandfather say, "Ideas have consequences." This was the first time he had experienced it for himself. Could he not have his family's property as well as his politics?

"For your mother's sake can you stay home for at least a month? I wish this visit to be a happy and memorable one for her."

"Yes, sir."

There was a knock on the office door. "Are you gentlemen going to talk all day? We are invited to the farm for a family get together," Abigail explained.

"That sounds wonderful. I am starving and I miss my family. I plan to be here for a month or two. I can write from here as easily as I can write in New York."

"That is wonderful!" she slipped her arm through his. "We have so much to get caught up on!"

Hannah and Benjamin stayed home that evening while Thaddeus and his parents walked to the farm. "You are a sight for sore eyes," Eli jovially greeted his cousin with a slap on the back.

"Your safe return home is an answer to our family's prayers," Daniel warmly welcomed.

"Eli, you have expanded the fields," Thaddeus observed.

"Now with the bridge, it is easy and profitable to expand on the western side of the river."

"Yes, but what do you do with the surplus?"

"We barter the surplus at the general store for what we cannot grow ourselves or sell it for cash. Of course my father always sees that no one in our church ever goes hungry."

"How is Aunt Grace doing?" Thaddeus had always enjoyed her entertaining stories about her childhood.

"Aunt Grace is busy writing a book on the history of Fryeburg and Sadie is busy painting scenes from Fryeburg," Eli explained. "Those two ladies are a creative pair."

"Thaddeus, we are so glad you are home," Rachel gave him a big hug.

"How is my cousin the proletariat?" he attempted a joke.

"I am not a proletariat and I certainly do not believe in that nonsense!" she quipped. "I chose to leave home and earn my own money. I have chosen to invest my inheritance in a business partnership. I am a business owner. I guess that would make me a bourgeoisie in your world."

Eli stifled a laugh. "Never argue with a Miller woman for you shall surely lose."

He looked at Rachel with a new found respect. "Perhaps I have been away from home too long."

"Mother's apothecary business is also very successful. She now sells her herbs at the general store," Eli added with pride.

"Do you mean she sells those plants that were always hanging in the kitchen to dry?"

"Yes and I had to expand her herb garden three times in three years. Isaac has become the apothecary's assistant. He has grown up quite a bit these past two years. Someday he will become quite the farmer."

"Or someday he may become quite the sawyer," Daniel added.

"Are you home permanently?" Eli had heard talk of Thaddeus taking over the law firm.

"I am only home for a month or two while I work on my manuscript on the California Gold Rush. Then I plan to live in Europe researching and writing."

"When will you return?" Rachel asked.

He shrugged. "A journalist must be free to follow his story."

Kate stood in the door and called, "Supper is ready!"

"No one needs to call me twice!" Thaddeus laughed as he and his cousins headed to the house.

XVIII

Fire!

Early the next morning the entire village stood silently staring at the smoldering ruins of what had been Fryeburg Academy. "Make way for the Senator," someone called as he pointed to Benjamin's carriage slowly heading towards the crowd. People respectfully parted so the carriage could stop directly in front of the ruins. Someone held the reins of the horses as Joshua and Abigail helped Benjamin and Hannah down.

Jacob and Eli followed the carriage on horseback. The Miller's farm wagon, driven by Kate and carrying the rest of the family, pulled to a stop on the other side of the street. The family stood together trying to comprehend the loss.

"The school is completely gone!" Isaac shook his head in disbelief. He had been excited about entering the Academy in the fall.

"Nonsense!" Benjamin retorted. "The school is the students and the faculty. The building is gone. That is all."

"What will we do about the building?" Isaac asked his grandfather.

"We rebuild, of course. In brick," he added.

The distraught principal, Alvin Boody, approached Benjamin. "This is terrible, simply terrible."

"Was anyone injured?" Hannah asked in alarm.

"No. Not that I know," Mr. Boody replied.

"There is nothing more we can do here. Mr. Boody, please inform the other Trustees that there will be a meeting in my office at three o'clock. We shall find another venue for the summer semester.

I believe, however, that the Village School is still standing," Benjamin smiled at his youngest grandson as a group of younger students and their parents scurried off.

Peter raced to reopen the general store before the crowd heading in that direction arrived. Two dozen town folk loitered on the store's front porch talking excitedly.

"I heard that fire was set,"[1] someone accused.

"Are you speaking of arson?"

"Who would do such a thing?" one woman gasped.

"It is not Christian- like to start malicious rumors," Reverend Hurd warned.

Thaddeus elbowed his way through the crowd. "Why would someone want to do that?" he questioned.

"Thaddeus, when did you get into town?" Reverend Hurd asked as he shook his hand.

"Yesterday afternoon."

"Are you going to write an article on the fire for your fancy New York City newspaper?" Mr. Bradley asked.

"It depends upon the story. Why would anyone want to burn down the school? If you know why, you will soon discover who."

"I heard there has been trouble between certain persons and a teacher," Mr. Weston suggested.

"That is a rumor," Mr. Abbott countered. "Just because certain people have had words, does not mean they would deliberately set a fire."

"It could have been done by someone passing through town," Mr. Osgood proposed.

"Or by a suspicious character returning home after a long absence," Mr. Weston joked.

"I have an alibi! I kept Darian up half the night with my snoring," Thaddeus laughed.

"Benjamin, I hope this will not be too much exertion for you," Hannah worried.

He affectionately patted his wife's hand. "What would I do without you? It is only a meeting in my office. I think I am still capable of shuffling down the hall, sitting and talking," he replied. He picked up a quill, "I need to write an agenda. There are many details to attend to."

Hannah realized as unfortunate as this event may be, it had given her husband a new purpose and a new project to which to devote himself. She smiled as she remembered an earnest, young headmaster devoted to his lesson plans. Was it really fifty nine years ago? Now this young headmaster had grown to the elder statesman and head trustee.

A few minutes before the clock on the mantel struck three, a dozen gentlemen arrived by foot or carriage at the front door of Benjamin's home.

"Thank you for coming on such short notice," Joshua greeted as he led them to the office where Benjamin was already seated. Abigail had the pewter tea pot set on the table and began to pour tea into the gold- rimmed ivory cups.

"Gentlemen, I trust there will be no objections that I have invited Mr. Boody and Reverend Hurd to our Trustee meeting," Benjamin began. "Our first order of business is to find a suitable venue for the summer semester."

"Since the Lord has blessed us with our new church building I would like to offer the use of our old Meeting House. It is available and a short walk from the academy."[1]

"How much rent will you require?"

"Not one cent. Our vestry is available as well,"[2] the good pastor offered.

"The Trustees are most grateful for your generosity. Our second order of business is to replace the books. Mr. Boody, could you please draw up a list of the destroyed books and the cost of replacing said books?"

"Yes, sir!" The young principal was overwhelmed by the enormity of the task before him.

"I do not believe it will be feasible to purchase new books by summer semester. Perhaps if we peruse our personal libraries we may loan or donate enough textbooks."

"What about desks?" Mr. Boody asked.

"I shall ask the congregation Sunday morning for donations of tables, chairs and desks," Reverend Hurd volunteered.

"Very well. Now that our immediate needs have been met, let us begin the task of rebuilding the school.

First we must hire an architect to draw up the plans. I would like to recommend Mr. Gridley James Fox Bryant of Boston. He has designed custom houses, government buildings, churches, school houses and private residences.[3] Does anyone else have a recommendation? I shall write to Mr. Bryant this evening."

"Sir, there has been talk that the fire was set."

"It was allegedly set," Benjamin corrected. "I make a motion that the Trustees offer a $200.00 reward for information concerning the fire.[4] Our concerns are solely to rebuild the academy. We shall reconvene upon the receipt of the building plans."

Summer semester commenced on schedule with borrowed books and second hand furniture in the midst of needless fears that the arsonist would strike again. Although the authorities questioned a few suspects no one was charged with a crime.[5]

Emily greeted Darian at the back door. "What a pleasant surprise! Is this a business or social visit?"

"It is a little of both," he replied evasively.

"Do you wish to speak to Danny?"

"I wish to speak to both of you," he said nervously.

"Then come join us for lunch." Emily placed another plate and some silverware on the table. "We have plenty of chicken and fiddleheads," she offered.

"Mr. Daniel, sir," he began.

"Please call me Danny. After three years I hope you think of me as an older brother."

"Danny, I do not want to go to the Academy in the fall. I have spent enough time in school already. I can read and write and do arithmetic well enough. I do not need to read Shakespeare or learn Latin. I need to learn a trade."

"That sounds very reasonable," he agreed. "What trade do you wish to pursue?"

"I want to work with you at the mill. I am not afraid of hard work. I could live in the bunk house."

"You most certainly will not!" Emily stated emphatically. "You will live here with us."

"I can use an apprentice. If you will agree to work for me until you are twenty-one I will teach you everything I know about the business. I cannot pay you much but you will have free room and board."

"We can put an extra bed and some furniture in the loft," Emily suggested eagerly.

"Will you force me to go to church?"

Daniel paused. "There will be no working on Sundays. You will come to town with us and keep the Sabbath with Nana. I will expect you to come to prayer meeting and Bible study here on Wednesday evenings with the rest of the employees."

Darian sighed with relief. "I can live with that. I am not sure how to tell Mr. and Mrs. Miller. I do not wish to appear ungrateful for all that they have done for me."

"I will talk to Grandpa and Nana. I think they will understand."

Instead of attending Fryeburg Academy, Darian Flynn would help rebuild it.

One hot July morning Abigail answered the front door to Peter Evans holding a small parcel. "I have a special delivery to the Honorable Benjamin James Miller from G.J.F. Bryant from Boston. Rachel insisted that I deliver this immediately."

"Papa the plans have arrived!" she cried excitedly.

A second Trustee meeting was held the next evening with the men poring over the details. "It is much bigger than necessary," one suggested.

"The town is growing. Look at the increased numbers of the younger children in the elementary schools. The academy may appear to be large when it reopens, but it will not be too large ten years from now.

I remember my first day of teaching when the academy opened in a one room school house in 1792. The second building we built in 1806 felt enormous in comparison. Yet even that building soon grew crowded."

"How much shall this cost?" another asked skeptically.

"I have budgeted $8,000,"[6] Benjamin stated.

"There are no brick yards in Fryeburg," another pointed out.

"With the board's permission I will ask Mr. Ammi Cutter of Lovell[7] for an estimate. His brick yard is the nearest one to Fryeburg," Benjamin stated.

"What of the lumber?"

"Would your grandson give us a discount for the lumber?"

"Some may call it nepotism," Benjamin warned.

"Yes, I am sure some will. However, I call it good business to use the largest, most successful lumber mill in town."

"With the board's permission I will ask Daniel for an estimate of the cost of lumber. We will meet again when we have the figures."

Daniel was so engrossed in calculating the board feet of oak for the school's flooring he did not hear Thaddeus enter his shop.

"This fire is a boom for business, is it not?" Thaddeus smirked.

"Are you here to purchase lumber or are you here to harass me?" Daniel replied.

"Neither. I am here to discuss a dilemma."

Daniel put down his quill and motioned for his cousin to take a seat. "I always thought you would be a minister. Why did you become a sawyer?"

"It is not an either or situation. All Christians are called to be a minister of the Gospel. Why did I become a sawyer? Why did Eli become a farmer? Why did you become a journalist?

I guess I like the smell of saw dust better than the smell of manure," he joked. "Seriously, God created these majestic trees. Each kind was designed perfectly for a certain job. I provide the perfect lumber to the builders and craftsmen. There is a certain sense of satisfaction knowing when I drive over Weston's Bridge or worship in the new church building, or walk past someone's home that I cut the lumber."

"Did you ever think about leaving town? I know Eli would never leave because he is going to inherit the farm. Why would you stay?"

"My family is here – my grandparents and parents."

"Yes, but you have siblings who could help care for your grandparents and parents."

"Yes I do, but you do not," Daniel reminded.

"Do you think I am selfish?" Thaddeus challenged.

"Do you care what I think? Do you care what anybody thinks? What do you think?"

"I think I will leave for Europe by the end of the month."

"If you already made your decision, then why are you asking me what I think? Are you asking for my approval?"

"I am asking are you content here. Do you ever wonder what adventures may lie ahead outside of this sleepy little town?"

"Like gold or French wines? Contentment begins here," he pointed to his chest. "There is no contentment without a right relationship with God."

Thaddeus shook his head. "Danny, Grandpa disowned me."

"I cannot believe that."

"He is leaving the house to Isaac after my parents are gone."

"Why would he do that?" Daniel asked suspiciously. "I assumed that you would become a partner in the law firm and inherit the house."

"I turned down the offer. I need the freedom to travel and write."

"Grandpa did not disown you; he offered you his legacy and you rejected it! Isaac was his second choice. What are you searching for Thad? What or who is in Europe that you think will make you happy?"

"Danny, will you take care of my parents when they grow older?"

"Why me?"

"Because you are a man of your word."

"You make it sound as if you will never return. You know the family will always welcome you home but why must you leave?"

"I have three- year- old twin sons. I met their mother in Paris, but they live with their grandparents in Poland. That is why I must return to Europe."

"You must marry this woman and bring your family home."

"That is not possible. She is dead."

"Then bring your sons home. Why should they be deprived of the affections of their father and entire Miller clan?" Thaddeus shook his head. "What is the real reason?"

"The biggest story of the century is the rise of Marxism. I must be there to witness and write about it."

"Are you leaving to witness it or to follow it? You are wrong. The biggest story of the century will be a civil war in this country. Grandpa is convinced that it will happen within my lifetime."

"Will you see to it that my parents will be cared for?"

"Of course I will. But will I ever see you again?"

"I will return when your civil war breaks out."

Abigail was in tears as Thaddeus descended the front staircase with his packed bags. "When will you return home?"

"Mother, I promise I will be more faithful in writing. Europe is not like California. You know what my job is like. I cannot promise that I will be home at a certain time. If I did, you would only be disappointed."

Joshua took a deep breath and bit his lip. He would not quarrel with his son nor would he upset his wife. "God be with you," he embraced his son. Thaddeus picked up his two leather satchels and headed to the Oxford House to catch the next stage coach. Joshua knew he would never see his son again.

The trustees met once again in Benjamin's office. "Welcome. We have much to discuss this evening. In addition to the building plans, I have estimates for the bricks from Mr. Cutter and estimates for the lumber from Daniel." He passed the figures around the table. At this point we are on budget. However I am still waiting to hear about the windows from Portland. This may put us over budget. Does anyone have any comments or questions?"

"How long do you think it will take to complete the school?" someone asked.

"Mr. Cutter may be baking the bricks concurrently with Daniel cutting the lumber and the cabinet maker building the desks. As soon as we approve the budget, we may begin."

"Yes, but when will the school be completed?"

"My estimate is two years."

XIX

The Final Journey

One August evening, a well-dressed, middle aged gentleman and lady stepped down from the stagecoach in front of the Oxford House. The driver carried two trunks into the lobby.

"I am very sorry; sir, but we have no vacancies. The dedication of the new Fryeburg Academy is tomorrow and every available room in town is booked," the clerk apologized.

"I must tell you, we need to store these for only an hour or so. We shall return with a carriage and cart them off." The lady handed the young man a half dollar.

"Yes, mam. I will keep a close eye on them."

Benjamin was rereading his speech which he had prepared for the dedication. Realizing that this would be his last speech and legacy, he wanted it to be perfect. A warm summer breeze was blowing through the open windows. Grace briskly knocked on the office door and entered.

"Well, Benjamin it is finally finished."

"Indeed it is. I thought I would not live to see the day when the academy was completed. It was a long and arduous endeavor but the results speak for themselves."

"Benjamin, I am not speaking of the academy. I mean my books, *The Fryeburg Chronicles*. Now the town has its own written history." She placed four leather bound volumes on the desk.

"I did not think our little town had that much history," Benjamin mused.

"It does not. I embellished it with my own stories – the day the British troops took over my house in Boston, how you and Micah argued about Shays Rebellion and how Alden left to go build the Erie Canal. I added my stories to make it more interesting."

There was a knock on the front door.

"Grace, would you please answer that for me," he asked wearily.

"Libby! Alden!" Grace cried as she hugged her two children tightly. "What a surprise! What are you doing here?"

"Aunt Hannah wrote us months ago to invite us to the dedication. We wanted to surprise you," Libby explained as she wiped away her tears.

"Benjamin Miller, did you know about this?" Grace called over her shoulder.

Benjamin reached for his cane and tried to stand. As a wave of nausea and dizziness briefly overcame him he closed his eyes and tried to catch his breath.

"Benjamin?" Grace and Hannah followed by Libby and Alden ran into the office where they found a pale and trembling Benjamin.

"I fear I have over exerted myself. A good night's rest is all I need."

"Uncle Benjamin, please allow me to help you upstairs," Alden offered.

"Micah? You have come back?"

"Uncle Benjamin, it is your nephew, Alden. We have not seen each other for decades. Libby tells me all the time how much I look like my father."

"Of course. Welcome Libby and Alden. We shall visit tomorrow"

Benjamin was at his desk bright and early the next morning.

"Perhaps we shall forego the festivities this afternoon," Hannah suggested.

"I am fine dear. All I needed was a good night's sleep. I must rehearse my speech one more time. Benjamin chose to lie down and rest instead of eating lunch.

"Joshua, I have never seen Papa this weak and frail before," Abigail confessed.

"I know. He has aged greatly these past two years. After today he will have plenty of time to relax. Your mother was wise to move the party from here to the farm."

"Well you know how much Aunt Grace and Libby love to entertain."

"Benjamin, it is time to wake up and get dressed. The carriage is ready," Hannah shook him awake.

"Am I late for court?" he asked in a panic.

"Do you wish to be late for the dedication?" she took out his best suit from the armoire.

"I will be one of the first students to attend the new school in a few weeks," Isaac excitedly reminded his parents as they walked down the Main Street to the academy.

Alden drove the carriage carrying his mother and sisters. "I fondly remember my years as an instructress here," Libby reminisced.

"I fondly remember the pranks I pulled when I was a student here," Alden laughed.

Eli and Julia with their children made their way through the crowds. "Someday I will go to school here," Davy stated with pride.

Peter and Rachel closed the store early to attend the ceremony. As they strolled down the street Rachel invited, "The family is having a celebration at the farm later. Would you like to attend?"

Peter smiled broadly. Maybe he did have a chance after all. "I would be delighted. In fact I hope to spend more time with your family."

Daniel, Emily and Darian entered the foyer of the school. Darian proudly surveyed the oak floor for which he had helped cut the wood. He thought it was a shame that all those leather soles would scuff it up.

At five minutes before the hour, Joshua stopped the carriage in front of the school. Abigail took one more look over her shoulder.

"Thaddeus is not coming," Joshua said softly as he jumped out, assisted his wife and mother in-law down. "Take my hand, sir, and let Abigail and I help you down. I will park the carriage and meet you inside." He nodded to Hannah.

Hannah took her husband's arm while they stood at the foot of the granite steps, admiring the brick edifice trimmed with granite. "I have never been as proud of you as I am at this moment."

"Hannah, I could have never accomplished the things I have without you by my side."

"I know, dear," she smiled.

They slowly climbed the granite steps, passed through the broad front door and entered the spacious hall. To the right was the recitation room, to the left was the apparatus room and directly in front was a large school room. "I have studied those plans for months and to finally see this for myself," Benjamin whispered to himself.

"Papa, are you able to climb another flight of steps to reach the auditorium?" Abigail asked as she clutched his arm.

He ignored the heaviness he felt in his chest. With sheer determination he took one step at a time, stopping occasionally to catch his breath.

Joshua ran up to Reverend John Wilde, the main speaker, "Sir, Senator Miller is quite unwell. Would you be willing to let him speak first before slipping out the side door?" He looked out the second-story window where he spied Isaac waiting in the carriage.

Reverend Hurd greeted Benjamin as he arrived in the auditorium which held four hundred people. "Sir, we have arranged for you to speak first and sit by the exit. Please feel free to leave at any moment you feel weary."

The good pastor opened the dedication with a benediction. Benjamin mustered all of his strength, held his cane and rose from his chair. He approached the podium with the same poise and dignity as he had in the court room for decades. He carefully placed his ten page speech in front of him and looked out upon the sea of expectant faces.

"On this most auspicious occasion I shall impart decades' worth of scholarship. 'The fear of the Lord is the beginning of knowledge: but fools despise wisdom and instruction.'" He folded his speech and slowly walked back to his seat.

Discreetly, Joshua knelt by the side of his chair. "Mrs. Miller wishes to return home with you now."

"How wise of her. Yes, I do believe I need a rest before the festivities." Joshua escorted him outdoors where Hannah and Isaac were waiting in the carriage.

"It was your finest hour," Hannah squeezed his hand.

Joshua and Isaac helped Benjamin into the house. "Sir, would you like to take a rest upstairs?"

"No, thank you. I wish to speak to my grandson in my office."

Isaac sat in the large wingback chair across from the desk. "When I was your age I did not have any friends. These were my friends." He pointed to the books lining two walls of book cases. I am appointing you and your heirs as the guardians of these books. When I lived in Philadelphia, Benjamin Franklin established a social library where members paid dues and shared their books with one another. Someday Fryeburg shall have a library. When that day comes, you will donate these books."

"Do I have to read them all?"

"No, just give them away."

Isaac brightened. "I can do that!"

"Today I am giving you my desk. It once belonged to Aunt Grace's father who imported it from England before the Revolutionary War. When I was your age, I would read and write at the desk dreaming of the day I would become a lawyer like John Adams. Aunt Grace gave this to me as a wedding gift."

"Grandpa, what about that?" he pointed to the large ink stain. He never understood why his grandfather never bought himself a new desk.

"I was a prideful and arrogant young man who demanded that his only son be just like me. Only the Lord created him with the talents and patience to be a successful farmer and not with the love of books and writing. No matter how hard your father tried to please me, it was never good enough. One day he accidentally spilled some ink when practicing his penmanship. This stain reminds me of my sin and the need for forgiveness. This is how I wish for you to remember me – a sinner in need of forgiveness.

I fear Thaddeus will not be returning to Fryeburg. Therefore I have left this house to you after the passing of my daughter Abigail."

"Grandpa!" he gasped.

Benjamin lifted his hand to silence him. "I am very tired now. It is all in the will. Please tell your grandmother I need her."

"Yes, Grandpa."

The pain in his left arm was excruciating. He struggled to take a breath. He had to tell Hannah where he hid those papers. No one must ever find them!

Isaac left for the kitchen where he found his aunt and uncle speaking in whispers. "Where is Nana?"

"She is upstairs resting," Abigail explained.

The Final Journey

"Grandpa needs her."

She nodded and wearily climbed the stairs to get her mother.

"Benjamin, I am here," Hannah smiled as she saw her husband sleeping in his chair. She gently shook him. "Let us get you upstairs where you can get a proper rest. Benjamin?" she shook him again. "Benjamin!" she screamed.

There was no reply. Benjamin James Miller had made his final journey from home.

Fryeburg Landmarks

F**ryeburg Academy** founded in 1792 it is one of the oldest private schools in the United States serving a widely diverse population of local day students and boarding students from around the world. www.fryeburgacademy.edu

This is a sketch of Fryeburg Academy built in 1806 and burned in 1851

1913 photo of Fryeburg Academy built in brick after the wooden structure burned in 1851. It still stands today and serves as the main building.

The Judah Dana House was built in 1816 on the corner of River Street and Main Street by Judah Dan, the first attorney in Fryeburg and Oxford County. Senator Dana's career was the inspiration for Benjamin Miller's life. In 1956 this historic home was torn down to make way for the Fryeburg Post office. Several local children entered the granite-lined tunnel which went under Main Street to the former Eckley Stern's residence across the street. According to oral tradition this home was part of the Underground Railroad. This is the location for the fictional Benjamin Miller's house.

The First Congregational Church of Fryeburg, located at 655 Main Street, was dedicated in July of 1850 and continues to serve as a house of worship today.

The Oxford House has been part of Fryeburg's history since James and Abigail Osgood rented out rooms in their Main Street home. Over the decades the building expanded many times before burning in February 1887. The Oxford Hotel, a grand 100 room hotel, was built in its stead. Unfortunately it too burned to the ground in 1906. Today the Oxford House Inn is a country inn and gourmet restaurant built on a portion of the site of the hotel.

An undated photo of the Oxford House taken before 1887

Weston's Covered Bridge was designed by Paul Paddleford and built in 1844 on the banks of Weston's Farm to span the Saco River. It was lost in a high Spring flood in 1957.

This stone building first served as the Village school house. Today it is the Fryeburg Public Library

Discussion Questions and Research Projects.

1. Hundreds of thousands of Irish immigrated to the United States and Canada during the Great Hunger of the 1840's. Was the Irish Potato Famine a natural or manmade disaster? Support your reasons. What kind of reception did they receive from the Boston populace? These new immigrants were Catholic while the vast majority of the New England population was Protestant. What role did religion play in the Irish communities? Do you know anyone of Irish descendant? When and from where did their ancestors emigrate? Name two U.S. Presidents of Irish descent.
2. Hannah Miller did not buy coffee or white sugar because she did not wish to support slavery. Can one person's consumer habits make a difference? Explain your answer.
3. Slavery did not begin with the American colonies nor did it end with the Civil War. List some past civilizations which practiced slavery. Where in the world is slavery practiced today? Visit the following websites for more information: www.thepolarisproject.com and www.notforsalecampaign.com.
4. List the ten tenets of Karl Marx's *Communist Manifesto*. Do you agree with any of his ideas? If so,

which ones? Do you disagree with any of his ideas? If so, which ones? What was Marx's view of religion? What was his view of the family?

5. Describe the economics practiced at Evans' General Store. By what three methods could a customer obtain goods?

6. What segment of society originally flocked to the textile mills for employment? What impact would this have on the family? What were some of the reactions to Rachel's announcement that she was moving to Biddeford to work in a mill? Describe the working conditions then. Do you know anyone who worked in a textile mill? Compare their working conditions to Rachel's.

7. The Millers read *The Last of the Mohicans*, *Moby Dick* and *The Scarlett Letter*. Research each author of these American classics.

8. Thaddeus disappointed his family when he chose to pursue his own career. Do you agree or disagree with his choice. Explain your answer.

End Notes

I
The Millers
1. John S. Barrows, <u>Fryeburg, Maine An Historical Sketch</u> (Fryeburg, Maine: Pequawket Press, 1938) p. 84.
2. David McCullough, <u>John Adams</u> (New York: Simon & Schuster, 2001) pg. 76
3. Barrows p. 91
4. Barrows p. 126

II
The Journey from Ireland
1. Robert I Weiner, <u>The Long 19th Century: European History from 1789 to 1917</u> (Chantilly, VA: The Teaching Company Course Guide Book, 2005) pg. 37
2. Ibid
3. Ibid
4. www.historyplace.com/worldhistory/famine/
5. Ibid
6. Ibid
7. Ibid
8. Ibid
9. Jeremy Thornton, <u>The Irish Potato Famine: Irish Immigrants Come to America 1845-1850</u> (New York: Rosen Publishing Group, 2004) p.1
10. www.historyplace.com/worldhistory/famine/

11. Thornton, pg. 1
12. Thornton, pg. 13
13. Thornton, pg. 68
14. www.historyplace.com/worldhistory/famine/
15. Ibid
16. Ibid
17. Ibid
18. Ibid
19. Ibid
20. Thornton, pg. 115
21. Ibid
22. Ibid
23. Ibid
24. Thornton, pg. 100
25. Thornton, pg. 101
26. Ibid

III
Saturday on the Farm

1. Steven E. Woodworth, <u>Manifest Destinies: America's Westward Expansion and the Road to the Civil War</u> (New York: Alfred A. Knopf, 2010) p. 300
2. Woodworth, p. 302
3. www.wikipedia.en/wiki/London_Bridge

IV
Keeping the Sabbath

1. www.biography.com/people/St.Patrick-9434729
2. Gary Amos and Richard Gardiner, <u>Never Before in History</u> (Richardson, TX: Foundation for Thought and Ethics, 2004) pg.14-15
3. Amos, pg. 39
4. Woodworth, p. 48-53
5. Woodworth, p. 299
6. Woodworth, p. 40
7. Woodworth, p. 41-43

V
The Journey to Buffalo
1. Woodworth, p. 41
2. www.enwikipedia.org/wiki/Buffalo_NewYork
3. Woodworth, p. 42
4. Woodworth, p. 43
5. Ibid
6. Ibid
7. Woodworth, p. 46
8. Woodworth, p. 306
9. Woodworth, p. 307
10. Ibid

VI
Karl Marx
1. The Communist Manifesto pg. 79
2. Marx, p. 87
3. Marx, p. 95
4. Marx, p 96
5. Marx, p 96-97
6. Marx, p. 100
7. www.en.wikipedia.org/wiki/The_Communist_Manifesto pg. 79
8. Ibid

VII
The General Store
1. Bobby Kalman, Early Stores and Markets (New York: Crabtree Publishing Company, 1992)
2. Henry F. Graff, Editor, The Presidents A Reference History (New York: Simon & Schuster Macmillan, 1997
3. Woodworth, p. 298
4. Woodworth, p. 301
5. Woodworth, p. 304

VIII
The Journey to Biddeford
1. McCullough, p. 293
2. Barrows, p. 273

IX
The Boarding House
1. www.secondcongregationalchurchinbiddeford.org.
2. www.biddefordmaine.org/index.asp
3. Donald Guillerault, Biddeford Mill Tour Guide, August 27, 2013
4. William Moran, <u>The Belles of New England: The Women of the Textile Mills and the Families Whose Wealth They Wove</u> (New York: St. Martins Griffin, 2004) pg. 14
5. Moran, pg.16

X
The Textile Mill
1. Moran, p.21-22
2. www.biddefordmaine.org/index.asp
3. Guillerault, mill tour

XI
Life without Rachel
1. Barrows, p. 34
2. Barrows, p. 35

XII
The Sawyer
1. Eric Sloane, <u>Eric Sloane's America</u> (New York: Promontory Press, 1982) p. 45
2. p. 29
3. Sloane, p. 27
4. Sloane, p. 25
5. Sloane, p. 27
6. Ibid

End Notes

XVI
Just a Farmer

1. www.wikipedia.org/wiki/Millard_Fillmore
2. Fryeburg Fair Book Committee, The Fryeburg Fair First 150 Years 1851-2000 (West Oxford Agricultural Society, 2000) p. 17
3. Fryeburg Fair Book Committee, p. 18
4. Ibid
5. Fryeburg Fair Book Committee, p. 221

XVII
The Journey from California

1. Woodworth, p. 322
2. Woodworth, p. 323
3. Ibid
4. www.wikipedia.org/wiki/Karl_Marx
5. Marx, p. 17
6. Marx, p. 22
7. Marx, p. 24
8. Marx, p. 23
9. Marx, p. 25

XVIII
Fire!

1. Barrows, p. 128
2. Ibid
3. June Wilkinson, "The Middle Years" The Fryeburg Academy Sesquicentennial 1792-1942 Booklet
4. Ibid
5. Barrows, p. 128
6. Ibid
7. David Crouse, "Ammi Cutter 1819-1896 Builder & Entrepreneur" (Bangor, ME: Cold River Chronicle Issue #60, April 2012)

Bibliography

Books:
Amos, Gary and Gardiner, Richard. Never Before in History. Richardson, TX. Foundation for Thought and Ethics. 2004
Barrows, John S. Fryeburg, Maine An Historical Sketch. Fryeburg, ME, Pequawket Press. 1938.
Fryeburg Fair Book Committee. The Fryeburg Fair First 150 Years 1851-2000. West Oxford Agricultural Society. 2000.
Graff, Henry F., Editor, The Presidents A Reference History. NY. Simon & Schuster Macmillan. 1997.
Kalman, Bobby. Early Stores and Markets. NY. Crabtree Publishing Company. 1992.
Marx, Karl. The Communist Manifesto.
McCullough, David. John Adams. NY. Simon & Schuster. 2001
Moran, William. The Belles of New England: The Women of the Textile Mills and the Families Whose Wealth They Wove. NY. St. Martins Griffin. 2004.
Sloane, Eric. Eric Sloane's America. NY. Promontory Press. 1982.
Thornton, Jeremy. The Irish Potato Famine: Irish Immigrants Come to America 1845 – 1850. NY. Rosen Publishing Group. 2004.
Weiner, Robert I. The Long 19th Century: European History from 1789 to 1917. Chantilly, VA. The Teaching Company Course Guide Book. 2005.

Woodworth, Steven E. <u>Manifest Destinies: America's Westward Expansion and the Road to the Civil War.</u> NY. Alfred A. Knopf. 2010.

Articles:
Crouse, David. "Ammi Cutter 1819-1896 Builder & Entrepreneur". <u>Cold River Chronicles.</u> Issue # 60. Bangor, ME. April 2012.
Wilkinson, June. "The Middle Years". <u>The Fryeburg Academy Sesquicentennial 1792-1942.</u> Booklet.

Websites:
www.biddefordmaine.org/index.asp
www.enwikipedia.org/wiki/Buffalo_NewYork
www.en.wikipedia.org/wiki/The_Communist_Manifesto
www.historyplace.com/worldhistory/famine/
www.secondcongregationalchurchinbiddeford.org
www.wikipedia.en/wiki/London_Bridge

Interview/Tour:
Donald Guillerault, Public Tour Guide. Biddeford Mill Tour, August 27, 2013.

CPSIA information can be obtained
at www.ICGtesting.com
Printed in the USA
LVOW01s1549090816
499664LV00016B/556/P